Ballerina Weather Girl

NOT-SO-
ORDINARY
GIRL

Ballerina Weather Girl

By Shawn K. Stout
Illustrated by Angela Martini

Previously published as
Fiona Finkelstein, Big-Time Ballerina!!

Aladdin
New York   London   Toronto   Sydney   New Delhi

ALADDIN

An imprint of Simon & Schuster Children's Publishing Division

1230 Avenue of the Americas, New York, NY 10020

This Aladdin paperback edition May 2013

Text copyright © 2009 by Shawn K. Stout

Illustrations copyright © 2009 by Angela Martini

Originally published as *Fiona Finkelstein, Big-Time Ballerina!!*

All rights reserved, including the right of reproduction in whole or in part in any form.

ALADDIN is a trademark of Simon & Schuster, Inc.,

and related logo is a registered trademark of Simon & Schuster, Inc.

Also available in an Aladdin hardcover edition.

For information about special discounts for bulk purchases,

please contact Simon & Schuster Special Sales at 1-866-506-1949 or

business@simonandschuster.com.

The Simon & Schuster Speakers Bureau can bring authors to your live event.

For more information or to book an event contact the Simon & Schuster Speakers Bureau at

1-866-248-3049 or visit our website at www.simonspeakers.com.

Designed by Jessica Handelman

The text of this book was set in Perpetua Std.

Manufactured in the United States of America 0414 OFF

2 4 6 8 10 9 7 5 3

Library of Congress Control Number 2012946429

ISBN 978-1-4424-7401-7 (pbk)

ISBN 978-1-4424-7402-4 (hc)

ISBN 978-1-4424-7403-1 (eBook)

For my mother, Patricia Beard,

and for the nice old lady in the hall

For my mother, Patricia Beard,

and for the nice old lady in the hall.

• Chapter 1 •

Fiona Finkelstein could not believe her eyes.

After all, eyes could sometimes play tricks on you. That was a flat-out fact. She had seen that happen to a man on TV once. He got lost in the desert and was awful thirsty. He thought he saw a glass of lemonade by a pool in the distance. So he kept on walking and walking. But there wasn't any lemonade or any pool. Just sand that went on forever and ever.

That was how tricky eyes could be.

Fiona wasn't sure her eyes were the trick-playing kind. But you could never be too careful. So she stared at the notice on Madame Vallée's Brag Board until her eyes crossed and the words turned to fuzz.

"Do you see what that says?" Cleo asked, pulling on Fiona's arm. "Now remember, you swore you wouldn't go all nutty."

"I know. I know." Fiona gulped to keep back the mighty storm brewing in her stomach. She couldn't look away. Not even with Cleo yanking on her arm. If only Fiona hadn't locked pinkies with her best friend and sworn she wouldn't go all nutty.

Do not go nutty, do not go nutty, do not go nutty.

Fiona really wanted to be excited like Cleo. And part of her *was* excited. A small part, deep down inside. Way, way down. Unfortunately, that part was being squashed by the part of her that was ready to throw up.

Because this is what was written on the piece of paper:

LA PETITE ACADEMY TO DANCE IN

The Nutcracker!

The Maryland Ballet Company

has invited

Madame Ursula Vallée's

La Petite Ballet Academy to

dance in their production of

The Nutcracker.

The performance will take place

on Sunday, December 15

at the historic

Grande Metropolis Theatre

in Ordinary, Maryland.

○ ○ ○ ○

But *this* is how Fiona read it:

Fiona Finkelstein,

this is your chance to be
a big-time ballerina. Your chance
to dance on a real stage!
With a real curtain! It's just what
you've always wanted. But there
will be lots of people staring at you,
Fiona. What if you forget your steps?
What if you throw up in front
of everyone again? No one wants to
see that. Quick, think of how you are
going to get out of this one!

○ ○ ○ ○

"Fiona," Cleo said, still tugging on her arm.
Cleo sounded far away. Like she was standing

on the other side of that desert right beside the glass of lemonade. Like maybe in Australia, which is where Fiona thought she might like to be at that very moment, hiding in a kangaroo's pouch.

All she could think about was that *one* recital. The one when her stage fright first showed up. The one when she threw up all over Benevolence Castle's cancan costume. And what's worse, Benevolence happened to be wearing it at the time.

Fiona remembered all of those strange people staring at her. The audience. She remembered how the brain suckers had come and vacuumed up all of the dance steps from her memory. And she remembered how she felt when the tornado in her stomach started to twist. And then how the macaroni and cheese and baked beans she had for dinner were suddenly all over the stage. Well . . . over Benevolence, really.

And how Benevolence screamed.

Fiona remembered, all right. It played over and

over in her head like a terrible TV commercial. Like the one annoying commercial where the lady has a headache and the baby is crying and the kids are yelling and the alarm clock is going off and all the lady needs is a dip in a bubble bath to make it all stop. It was just like that. But without the bubble bath.

Fiona felt a squeeze on her shoulder, and she was suddenly back in ballet class. She looked up and saw Madame Vallée smiling down at Cleo and her. Her face looked as smooth as a porcelain doll's.

"Ladies, time to begin," said Madame Vallée sweetly.

After a moment, Fiona turned to follow Cleo into the practice room. Madame Vallée rested her hand gently on Fiona's shoulder and walked along beside her.

"Worry gives the small things a big shadow," Madame Vallée said. "It's best to stay in the sun, Fiona dear."

"Okay," said Fiona. But she wasn't sure what she was saying okay to. Madame Vallée sometimes said the kind of things that didn't make a lot of sense.

"Ah," said Madame Vallée, "You remind me of

myself as a little girl. Always running away from the bear in the woods. You must learn to stop running. You have to face the bear and teach it to dance. Yes?" She gave Fiona's shoulder a squeeze.

Fiona had an inkling of what Madame Vallée was trying to tell her. Well, at the very least she was sure it didn't really have to do with dancing bears. Trying to figure out Madame Vallée's riddles was like trying to crack open a geode. You had to take several hard whacks at it before you could see the sparkly crystals inside.

Madame Vallée glided to the front of the practice room. Everything about her was fancy. She wore flowery ribbons on her pointy black shoes and dolphin-blue sparkles above her eyes. She even spelled her name fancy. The letter e was in her name two times, and the first one, the one right after the l, had a fancy spark shooting out of it.

Last summer, Fiona had decided that her own name could be fancied up a bit. But why stop with just one spark from just one **e**? Fiona wanted to decorate her name like an exploding firecracker on the Fourth of July: **Fìóña**. Who wouldn't like a fancy name like that?

Mr. Bland, Fiona's fourth-grade teacher, that's who. He didn't want to see her name in fireworks at the top of her homework assignments. So she had to go back to writing it the regular old boring way. Without even the tiniest spark.

"Now, ladies, come sit here." Madame Vallée pointed to the area on the floor by the CD player.

Cleo grabbed the sleeve of Fiona's leotard and pulled her down so they were sitting side by side, cross-legged. Fiona could hear Benevolence Castle and her two sisters, Beatrice and Bonnie (the Three Bees), buzzing behind her.

"Move in closer," said Madame Vallée, motioning with her arms. "Scoot on your *derrières*. That's it."

Derrière. Who knew that your rear end could sound so fancy?

Fiona felt a foot in her backside as she scooted in closer. "Move it, Vomitstein."

Benevolence scowled at her. Fiona scowled right back and then faced the front of the room.

Madame Vallée was waving one arm dramatically in a circle. It ended in a point. "You have all seen the Brag Board today. *Oui?*"

Fiona folded her arm over her stomach, trying to keep it calm.

"Yes!" came the squeals from everyone else.

"You saw that our little school, La Petite, has been invited to dance with the Maryland Ballet Company in *The Nutcracker*," said Madame Vallée.

Oohs and *ahhs* filled the room. The buzz of the Three Bees grew loud with excitement.

But the only noise that came from Fiona was her stomach. It gurgled.

"Yes, yes, yes, this is all very exciting business," Madame Vallée continued. "But what you do not know is that this class, your class, will dance the part of the angels."

"Wow! Angels!" Cleo shouted, elbowing Fiona. "She said angels!"

Fiona gripped her stomach tighter.

"Rehearsals start next week," said Madame Vallée. "Please bring your—"

"I don't remember any angels in *The Nutcracker*," interrupted Benevolence. "I've seen it three times. There are toys and dolls and rats. I remember those." She folded her arms across her chest.

"Yeah, rats," said Beatrice.

"Big ones," said Bonnie, curling her hands like claws and showing her teeth.

Benevolence elbowed Bonnie and shushed her. "So what kind of angels are we going to be, anyway?"

"The kind that wear haloes?" asked Beatrice.

"The kind that wear wings?" asked Bonnie.

Then Beatrice and Bonnie said together, "The kind that fly?"

Madame Vallée raised her eyebrows until her dolphin-blue sparkles disappeared behind her bangs. She put her hands on her hips. "The good kind of angels that do not ask so many questions."

This cracked everybody up. And if Fiona hadn't been in a really awful, worry-headed, tornado-bellied panic, she would have cracked up too.

That was a flat-out fact.

∘ Chapter 2 ∘

After ballet practice, Fiona trudged down Winter Street and across two blocks to Pepper Avenue toward WORD-TV news station. It took her twice as long to get there because trudging was very slow. Her feet, which were usually as light as marshmallows, felt as clunky as tomato soup cans.

While she trudged, Fiona did some thinking. She thought about all of the ballet recitals at La Petite that she had missed after that *one*. Of course, she had missed them for very good and acceptable reasons.

Like the time she couldn't dance because of a sudden spell of hiccups. (They weren't the quiet kind of hiccups either, the ones that you can sort of keep inside. They were the really LOUD kind of hiccups, the ones that BURST out and give you a JOLT.)

And the time she couldn't find her costume. Who would have thought to check inside Mrs. Miltenberger's mailbox?

And the time she caught a terrible, but fortunately brief, case of restless legs syndrome. And honestly, who can dance with restless legs?

But missing those plain old recitals didn't mean that much to Fiona. Those recitals weren't as big and important as *The Nutcracker*.

The Nutcracker! This was her chance to be a big-time ballerina. Just like the ones in the pictures that hung in the hallway of La Petite. Those ballerinas wore beautiful costumes and looked as light and feathery as Queen Anne's lace. Each one was in a perfect pose just like the ballerina figurines that Dad gave her on birthdays.

Being a big-time ballerina was Fiona's dream. But how could she do it when just the very thought of it made her stomach do its own kind of dance?

Butterflies, Fiona's mom called them. She said that everybody got them. Even her. She was an actress on the soap opera *Heartaches and Diamonds* and lived in California most of the time. So you'd think she would know. Butterflies, Fiona could handle. Butterflies like bombers were a different story.

When she finally reached the corner of Pepper and Mayfair, Fiona trudged her tomato soup can feet up the steps and through the front door of WORD-TV news station. Dad's office was down the hallway, fifth door on the left.

The door was open, but Dad wasn't inside. Fiona went in, anyway, dropped her ballet bag beside his desk, and shed her winter coat. She plopped into Turner—Dad's swiveling desk chair—to wait.

Turner was one of the best things about going to Dad's office. Fiona and her little brother Max could spend hours playing Around Around Until You're on the Ground. Turner sure could chuck you far.

But today, Fiona wasn't in the mood to be chucked. And besides, she didn't have her helmet and padding. So she rolled Turner closer to the desk and watched the green, yellow, and white blobs move across a map of Maryland on her dad's computer screen. By the looks of those blobs, Ordinary was going to be in for some rain tonight. That was one good thing about having a meteorologist for a dad—you got to know what the weather was going to be like before anybody else did.

But that was the *only* good thing about having a meteorologist for a dad.

Because everybody complained about weather. And some people—like Mr. Bland, for example—even blamed meteorologists for it. This made Fiona fume. Like her dad could actually *make* the weather.

Like he could place an order for three feet of snow. Or whip up a sunny day in a flash like a cook can whip up an order of dippy eggs and toast. That was just flat-out unfair.

"Hey, Dancing Bean," Dad said, appearing at the door in his dark brown suit and maroon tie. "This is a nice surprise. You've come to wish your old dad good luck?"

"Break a leg," Fiona corrected. Saying "good luck" was a surefire invitation for bad luck.

"I'll try," he said. He wiggled his leg around like it wasn't going to hold him up. "It does sort of feel wobbly." Fiona had heard that one before.

"I've got rehearsal in about five minutes," he said, "and I was just on my way to the dressing room. Want to tag along?"

Fiona shrugged. "I guess." She got up and followed him down the hall and into a tiny room with a stool, a rectangular table, and a large, oval mirror in a gold frame.

Dad sat down on the stool facing the mirror. Then he licked the tips of his fingers and patted down a sprig of hair at the back of his head. "So, Dancing Bean, how was your day?"

"Don't ask," Fiona said, watching his stubborn hair pop right back up again. "And this bean isn't in the mood to dance."

"Oh, really?" He pressed the hair down again, but it was fighting back. "Then what is this bean in the mood to do?"

"Here," Fiona said, "I'll do it." She licked the palm of her hand and then pushed his hair down flat. She held it steady. "Nothing," she said with a sigh. "Beans can't do anything. They're just beans."

"Tell that to the Mexican jumping bean," he said. And then he added, "Thanks, I bet that will do it. You can let go now."

Fiona pulled her hand away, and the sprig of hair stood up again. It was just asking to be yanked out by its roots. She grabbed for it, but Dad's hand got there first. "Leave it," he said, looking in the mirror and patting the stubborn hair. "I'm afraid it's an uphill battle." Then he winked at Fiona. "It's my fault. I shouldn't have teased it."

Dad stood up and smoothed out the front of his suit jacket. "So . . ."

Fiona breathed in deep and let out a big sigh. She carefully put in a little moan right at the end. She had recently learned how to do that from watching her mom on *Heartaches and Diamonds* and had been practicing the moaning part.

"Okay, let's have it," Dad said, turning to her.

She got ready to pour out everything that was sitting as heavy as bricks in her belly. "Well . . . ," she started.

"Well?" Dad fiddled with his tie once more. "How do I look?"

"Oh." *Obviously, the moaning part needs more practice.* "Pretty good, I guess."

Dad frowned playfully. "Hmmm, I was hoping for 'incredible,' but I guess I'll have to settle for 'pretty good.'"

"Norm, we'd better get started," said a man at the door. He was wearing rectangular glasses and long sideburns and had a clipboard tucked under his arm.

"I was just on my way," said Dad. "Gabe Durand, meet my daughter, Fiona."

"Hiya, Fiona," said Gabe.

"Gabe's the producer for the evening news," Dad explained.

Gabe patted Dad on the shoulder. "You must be pretty proud of your dad here. Promoted to chief meteorologist and about to do his first prime-time forecast." He shifted the clipboard under his arm. "That means more than a hundred thousand people will be watching him tonight."

Fiona's eyes got big. "A hundred thousand people?"

"At least," said Gabe. "And that's about a hundred thousand more than were watching his field reports during 'Wake Up with Weather.' No offense, Norm."

"None taken," said Dad, smiling. "I like to think of my 'Wake Up' fans as quality, not quantity."

Fiona turned to her dad. "Are you nervous?"

"Me? Nervous?" he said. "Never."

"Never?"

He smiled. And Fiona couldn't see one bit of nervousness in it.

"Want to watch the rehearsal?" asked Gabe. "We've got all new state-of-the-art equipment that's going to blow WYMD off the weather map."

"Can I, Dad?"

"I don't see why not." Dad picked up the phone on his desk and started dialing. "I'll ask Mrs. Miltenberger if she can pick you up, after. It's going to rain."

Fiona followed Gabe down a hallway and through a set of double doors into a wide, open room. Right away her eyes went to a gray desk, long and curved into a "C," and to the three giant cameras pointed right at it. They were the biggest cameras Fiona had ever seen. Much taller than Fiona, with thick wires and cables coming out from them.

"This is where it all happens," said Gabe. "Pretty cool, huh?"

Fiona nodded as she looked around. A line of clunky lights hung over her head. Off to the side, rows of TV sets were stacked on top of one another. And next to that, shelves of equipment with all kinds of silver buttons and knobs and dials. "Why did you get all of this new stuff?"

"Ratings. We're trying to compete with WYMD and other TV news stations," he said. "You know, to get more viewers."

"Oh." Fiona walked over to the desk. This was The Desk. Where Baxter Buckworth, the anchorman, sat every night to deliver the evening news.

She reached out with her finger to touch its smooth edge. "Is Baxter Buckworth coming to rehearsal?"

"Mr. Buckworth doesn't rehearse," said Gabe. And then he whispered, "He doesn't think he needs the practice. Besides, I think it interferes with his nap."

"His nap!" Fiona laughed out loud. Even *she* was too old for naps. As she rounded the long desk, Fiona noticed a large, blue screen against a wall in the far corner of the room. "What's that for?"

"*That* is part of what's going to make WORD News the most-watched weather forecast in the tristate region," said Gabe. "Why don't you try it out?" He flipped a switch on one of the cameras.

"For real?"

"Well, we aren't recording, and you won't be broadcasted out to one hundred thousand people. But you can pretend . . ."

"Okay," said Fiona. "Where do I stand?"

"Over there in front of the blue screen." Gabe

went to the back of the room and pressed a button on the wall. The clunky lights hanging above shone a spotlight on the screen, and the rest of the room went dark.

Fiona stepped into the spotlight and stared at the giant camera in front of her. She got into her TV showcase pose: one hand on her hip and the other one above her head, palm up. She lowered it to her side and then back up again.

"I'd like to buy a vowel," said Dad, appearing out of the darkness from behind the camera.

"Which one?"

"I've always liked 'u,'" he said.

"I like 'u,' too."

"Good one." Dad laughed.

Fiona dropped her arms to her side, stood up as tall and straight as she could, and flashed a smile.

"There you go," said Dad.

She looked at the screen behind her. "Where are all the maps?"

"See, a computer makes it so that, while watching at home, instead of this blue screen, all you see are maps behind me," said Dad. "Now, watch right here." He pointed to a TV that was facing Fiona on the other side of the camera.

"Where's the thingy you hold to change the maps?" she asked.

"Fiona, you really know your stuff," said Gabe.

Dad handed her a tiny remote control and showed her which button to push. Then, suddenly, Fiona was on the TV in front of her, standing in front of a big map of Maryland. She looked behind her, but the blue screen was still there. "Wow!"

She pushed another button on the remote-control gadget and a different map appeared behind Fiona on the TV. "Attention, Ordinary citizens, in case you haven't noticed, it's cold outside," she announced. Fiona clicked to the next map. "Get out your umbrellas and raincoats, because it's going to be a soggy one."

"She's a natural, Norm," said Gabe.

Fiona smiled. She spun around, cleared her throat, and then recited, "It's raining, it's pouring, Baxter Buckworth is snoring. He went to bed and bumped his head—"

"Finkelstein and Durand!" boomed a deep voice from the back of the room. "Is this a news station or a playground?" Fiona froze.

∘ Chapter 3 ∘

Mrs. Miltenberger plopped a bean and cheese burrito the size of a tennis shoe on Fiona's plate. She was the next-door neighbor, part-time Finkelstein babysitter, and honorary member of the Finkelstein family. "I never would have pegged Baxter Buckworth as a howler," she said, shaking her head. "He always seems to have such a pleasant demeanor on TV."

"Take it from me, when he's not on TV, his *duh* meaner is *duh* meanest," said Fiona, poking holes in the burrito with her finger. Baxter Buckworth's voice still echoed in her ears. About how EXPEN-SIVE the weather gadgets are and how they aren't KIDDIE TOYS and how this STATION is NO PLACE for children. Fiona had just stood there frozen in the eye of the storm, watching Dad and Gabe Durand get blown around by Hurricane Buckworth. "You should have seen his face," she told Mrs. Miltenberger. "It changed colors three times."

"Sounds like a regular circus act." Mrs. Miltenberger pulled out a chair across from Fiona and sat down. Then she waved her arms like she was fanning away bad air. "Let's just forget about old Barnum and Bailey Buckworth. This is your dad's big night on the seven o'clock news." She aimed the remote control at the small TV on the kitchen counter and clicked it on. "Where on earth is that brother of yours? If he doesn't get out here soon, I predict that a cold front will move in on his dinner."

Fiona shrugged and continued poking holes in her burrito until she made a Mr. Burrito Head— two holes for eyes, one for a nose, and ten for an oversize frown. Why should Mr. Burrito Head get to be happy?

Mrs. Miltenberger cleared her throat. "Max!" she shouted, startling Fiona.

In an instant, six-year-old Max leaped into the kitchen, arms raised above his head. He was wearing his usual outfit: swim trunks with seahorses all over them, goggles, a string of first-place medals for Ordinary's Pee-Wee Swim Team around his neck, and a beach towel cape.

"Oh, brother," groaned Fiona.

"Have a seat," said Mrs. Miltenberger. "You've almost missed your father's prime-time television debut, Max."

Max remained unmoved, posed like a statue of a superhero.

"Oh, for heaven's sake." Mrs. Miltenberger sighed but then corrected herself. "I mean, sit down, please, *Captain Seahorse*."

"I'd be happy to, ma'am," Max said in his best superhero's voice. And he slid into his chair, his cape swinging behind him.

"You'd be in big trouble if Dad was here," said Fiona.

"How come?" But Max didn't wait for an answer. He picked up his shoe-size burrito and stuffed an end of it into his mouth.

"Because Dad said that Captain Seahorse is an outlaw."

"Is not!" said Max, spitting chewed bean mush in all directions. "What's a outlaw?

"It's one of those bad men in the Westerns Dad watches on TV. You know, the ones with mustaches and real squinty eyes who are always at the saloon cheating at cards and starting gunfights," said Fiona.

Max squinted at Fiona.

"That's just how they look," she said.

"Actually," said Mrs. Miltenberger, wiping away bits of bean from her sweater, "I think what he said was that Captain Seahorse was outlawed from the dinner table. Not that he *is* an outlaw."

"Captain Seahorse has superstrong muscles for super swimming and fighting underwater forces of evil," announced Max. He gripped his burrito with both hands and squeezed so that beans oozed out both ends.

"All right, Captain Messy," said Mrs. Miltenberger, dislodging the burrito from his hands and handing him a pile of napkins. "Let's try eating your dinner and not strangling it."

Max and Mrs. Miltenberger wiped at his bean fingers. "Do outlaws have these?" he asked, pointing to the string of first-place medals around his neck.

Fiona looked at the bean-covered superhero. His goggles had fogged over, and he was trying to find his mouth with his fingers. She shook her head. How come Captain Strange Boy never seemed to get nervous when he swam in races with people watching?

Just then, the opening music for WORD-TV News 9 blared from the television. Fiona, Max, and Mrs. Miltenberger strained their necks toward the TV. Fiona couldn't wait to see her dad and his new weather show on the seven o'clock news: "Finkelstein's Fabulous Forecast."

She scooted her chair toward the TV for a better view. But when a close-up of Baxter Buckworth came on the screen, she cringed and backed up. "There he is. That's the hurricane."

"You'd never know by the looks of that smile," said Mrs. Miltenberger. "It's really something."

And it was. In each close-up, Baxter Buckworth's smile seemed bigger than the one before it. And it was full of white, sparkling teeth. Fiona had never seen such glistening white chompers. She wondered how he kept them so clean.

But before she could think too long about that, a picture of Fiona's dad flashed on the TV. "Now *there's* a handsome man," said Mrs. Miltenberger.

The announcer's voice boomed, "And 'Finkelstein's Fabulous Forecast' is up next."

"I'm done!" shouted Max, pushing his empty

plate to the center of the table. "I'm gonna watch Dad on the *big* TV." And in a flash, he was out of the kitchen.

"I've never seen a child eat so fast," Mrs. Miltenberger said, shaking her head. "Must be something about that outfit."

Fiona scooted her chair closer to the TV once more and waited for her dad to appear on the screen. When he did, Fiona and Mrs. Miltenberger clapped for him and then shushed each other so they wouldn't miss anything.

Dad stood in front of a huge map of Maryland, pointing to Ordinary and other towns nearby. Each town was marked with two clouds and a tiny sun peeking out from behind them.

Fiona watched him point from one town to the next on the map. She watched him arch and sweep his arms to show the polar air pushing across Maryland's panhandle. To Fiona's eyes, forecasting the weather looked a lot like dancing.

Her dad was dancing, in a weather-kind-of-way, in front of a hundred thousand people. And look at him. He was as cool as a Creamsicle.

Dad pointed to the cold temperatures across the state. "Get out your long johns," he said. "It's going to drop to thirty-four degrees in Ordinary, Waggerville, and Piedmont tomorrow."

He spun across the map of Maryland and moved his arms all around the Chesapeake Bay. He was flat-out good.

Dad moved on to the five-day forecast. "It looks like winter has definitely arrived," he said. "Look out for bitter temperatures by the end of the week."

"So be sure to bundle up out there," Dad said. "We're in for several cold days ahead." He smiled. "That's all for 'Finkelstein's Fabulous Forecast.' Back to you, Baxter."

Fiona clicked off the TV before Baxter Buckworth's face showed up again. She sighed and put a little moan right at the end.

Mrs. Miltenberger started clearing the table. "Well done," she said. "That was quite a weather report, delivered with authority and conviction. Just as it should be. He leaves no mystery about it. It's going to be *cold*."

"Mrs. Miltenberger," Fiona said, "if you knew that a hundred thousand people were watching you on TV, would you be nervous?"

"Me, on television? Why, I would be an utter wreck."

"Me too," admitted Fiona. "Dad said he wasn't, though. I mean, he said he wasn't nervous at all." And what about Mom? Acting in front of cameras and loads of people all the time. Even Max. He swam on a swim team in front of people all the time. And as far as Fiona knew, he hadn't ever thrown up on anybody. Why did he get all of the cool-as-a-Creamsicle genes?

Fiona couldn't understand it. "Why do you think he doesn't get nervous?"

"Oh. I don't know, maybe he is just one of those people who doesn't get all worked up about things."

That didn't help Fiona at all. She was one of those people who did get all worked up.

Mrs. Miltenberger continued, "Or maybe he uses one of those tricks to keep himself from getting nervous."

"Tricks?"

"You know, like picturing everybody in the room—or, in this case, the WORD-News 9 viewing area—in their underwear."

Underwear? Fiona thought about this. "How does that work?"

"Well, I've never tried it, personally," said Mrs. Miltenberger. "But I think if you picture something funny in your head, it's supposed to lighten up the situation. You know, and then you won't take whatever it is you're nervous about so seriously."

Fiona was filled with hope. And then all at once with dismay. Why hadn't anybody told her about this? She could have used this information a long time ago. Why were grown-ups always keeping these kinds of things to themselves? It was as if there were a treasure chest out there in the world with a big sign that said:

Everything you've ever wanted
to know about anything. Answers to
every problem. Just don't tell
Fiona Finkelstein!

Could this trick work for her? Could it get rid of her stage fright?

Maybe it all came down to one thing.

Underwear.

◦ Chapter 4 ◦

Right after Dad's weather report was over, Fiona dialed up California to give a report of her own. Mom answered on the third ring. "Hello, darling."

"We just watched Dad on TV for 'Finkelstein's Fabulous Forecast' in front of a hundred thousand people."

"Isn't that lovely," said Mom. "And how are you and Maxie? Anything new, wonderful, and exciting in Ordinary?"

"Not much," said Fiona. "It's raining here. And

I just wanted to tell you about Dad. That he did good and didn't mess up once."

"Good, that's good."

Fiona could hear papers rustling through the phone. "What's that noise?"

"I'm practicing my lines for tomorrow's taping. Scarlet pushes Nash Barrington off the deck of his yacht and makes off with a suitcase full of jewels."

"I thought Scarlet liked Nash," said Fiona.

Mom laughed. "No, darling. That was last week."

A kaleidoscope of underwear in all shapes, colors, and sizes spun in Fiona's mind that night. She couldn't sleep, too busy hatching out the particulars of Operation Underwear and too excited thinking about what it would mean if it worked.

She needed to test it, she decided. And for that, she needed people. Fortunately for her, she knew just the two for the job. But considering that it was the middle of the night, Fiona could only lie in bed and wait for them to get up.

Fiona watched the numbers on her nightstand clock move at a turtle's pace. How come time just creppetty-crept-crept along when she wanted it to go by fast? But when she wanted to stretch it out, time was a jackrabbit.

While the moonlight was still glinting off the frost on her bedroom window, Fiona couldn't stand it any longer. She switched on the lamp by her bedside, climbed out of bed, shivered, and wrapped her blanket over her shoulders. As she moved around her room she couldn't help but notice that her feet felt less clunky.

Fiona tried them out. She did *pirouettes* from her closet all the way to her dresser and back again. She did *jetés* around her bed. She smiled at her feet. "Pretty good," she said.

She did *chassés* in place, seven of them, jumping higher and higher, imagining that she was a Big-Time

Nutcracker Angel. *Chassé.* Onstage. *Chassé.* At the Grande Metropolis Theatre. *Chassé.* In front of an audience. *Chassé.* A really big audience. *Chassé.* With lots of people watching. *Chassé.* Too many people. *Chassé.*

"WHOA!" Fiona's last *chassé* went sideways and sent her crashing *derrière*-first into her dollhouse. She landed in the tiny living room on top of Banana, the miniature doll-dog retriever. "Ow."

"Do you know what time it is?" Dad was suddenly standing in the doorway. He yawned. "It's nighttime," he said, answering his own question. "Too late to be playing dollhouse."

"What's going on?" Max appeared beside Dad just then with his eyes closed and a bed buddy tucked under each arm.

"Nothing's going on. I . . ." Then Fiona realized something and smiled. "Hey, you're awake!"

"Not exactly," said Dad, yawning again.

And then she realized something else. "Hey,

you're in your underwear!" Fiona hadn't figured it would be this easy to test Operation Underwear. She wouldn't even have to do any imagining.

"Yes, Fiona. As I said, it's nighttime," said Dad. "How about going back to sleep with the rest of civilization?"

She looked at Dad in his boxer shorts and T-shirt and then at Max in his long johns. She folded her arms across her chest and waited for Operation Underwear to start working. Fiona wasn't sure what was supposed to happen. She thought that maybe she would feel all the nervousness that lived inside her just fly away.

But she didn't feel anything different. She felt the same as always. What went wrong?

"Earth to Fiona," said Dad.

"Huh?"

"I said, how about going back to sleep, Bean." Without waiting for an answer, Dad put his hand on Max's head and steered him back down the hallway.

Fiona wasn't going back to sleep. She couldn't. She was too busy trying to put the pieces of the Operation Underwear puzzle together. And then she smacked her forehead when she finally got it. How could she have missed it? She would have to be nervous for Operation Underwear to work. Nervous, just like she would be onstage.

By the time the sun finally got up, Fiona was already on the school bus telling Cleo all about Operation Underwear. "We have to find a way to make me nervous so I can try out the experiment," Fiona said, yawning.

"I know what," said Cleo. "You could stand up here with one foot on this seat and your other foot on that one." She pointed at the empty seat across the aisle. "And ride to school like that the whole way."

"You mean like a split?"

Cleo nodded, her eyes wide and daring. "That would make *me* nervous."

Fiona looked at all of the other kids on the bus.

That would be a lot of underwear to imagine. She stood up and faced them. Then she put her right foot on the seat across the aisle. When the bus changed gears, she lunged forward. Quickly, she slid back into her seat. "I want to be nervous, not killed." Fiona yawned again. "Keep thinking."

By the time they got to school, Fiona could barely keep her eyes open. The sleep she'd missed last night had caught up with her big-time.

Mr. Bland was filling up the blackboard with the day's vocabulary words when Fiona got to her desk. *Avoiding. Factories. Tight. Provoked.* She sank into her seat and propped her head up with her hands. It felt as heavy as a punch bowl.

She yawned and closed her eyes.

When she opened them again, the room was as quiet as an ice cube. And Mr. Bland was standing in front of her desk, staring down at her with a puckered brow.

She looked around the room. *Everyone* else was

staring at her too. Cleo's eyes were huge, and her face had gone pale. Fiona felt the color leave her own face, and she wanted to leave with it.

"Did we have a late night?" asked Mr. Bland.

"No." Fiona sat up straight in her chair and tried to look awake. "Well, um, sort of." She fought back another yawn.

"Are we suffering from insomnia?"

"Huh?"

"Insomnia," he said. "It's when you have trouble sleeping."

"Oh." Fiona hadn't known there was a name for it. "I guess if I'm in trouble for sleeping, then that's what I've got."

Everybody laughed, but Fiona wasn't trying to be funny. She thought she saw Mr. Bland's mouth curl into a smile. But then it was gone and his lips were pressed together again in a thin, tight line. Fiona's stomach churned.

"Do we need a call home to our parents?"

All this *we* talk was starting to confuse Fiona. Did he mean *her* parents? Or *his* parents? Did he *have* parents? "No, thank you," she said, hoping that good manners might save the day.

"Are you sure?" He stretched out the words so they sounded twice their size.

Fiona could feel everyone watching her, waiting

for what was going to happen next. Her heart started pounding. And then a grumble from her stomach gave her an idea. She thought about underwear.

Fiona concentrated. She imagined Mr. Bland in plain white ones. Like the kind they sell at the discount store in packs of twenty. As she was imagining this, Mr. Bland stood right beside her desk. And then Fiona couldn't help herself. The giggles came.

"Fiona Finkelstein," said Mr. Bland, "I fail to see the humor in this."

Fiona tried to stop the giggles. But it was like trying to stop a moving train. They kept coming and coming and getting stronger and louder. She looked around the room, anywhere but at Mr. Bland in his white underpants.

"I mean it, young lady," said Mr. Bland. "Settle yourself down, or we'll have to get Principal Sterling involved."

Fiona really was trying to settle herself down. She tried thinking about something unfunny. Chewed pencils. Rotten tomatoes. Finger in a mousetrap. Nothing worked.

Through the giggle tears that were now streaming down her face, Fiona looked at the chalkboard and concentrated on the day's vocabulary list. She said the words to herself and made up a sentence for each one. But the more she tried not to think about underwear, the more underwear crept into her brain.

AVOIDING: I am **avoiding** Mr. Bland and his underwear.

FACTORIES: **Factories** make things like cars, spoons, and underwear.

TIGHT: Mr. Bland wears **tight**ie whities.

That did it.

Fiona's giggles erupted full force and her shoulders began to shake. Around her, other kids started laughing then too. And that made it even worse. All Fiona could do was put her head down on her desk and give up. Which is what she did.

"Okay," Mr. Bland said with a sigh. "Fiona Finkelstein, to the principal's office. Now."

• Chapter 5 •

From the braces on her teeth to her round, red glasses, Principal Sterling was the very opposite of Mr. Bland. There was a sign on her office door that read: REMEMBER, THERE'S ALWAYS A PAL IN PRINCIPAL. So, even though Fiona had never been sent to the principal's office before, she wasn't scared. Besides, Principal Sterling had one of the nicest laughs Fiona had ever heard. It was like pennies splashing into a wishing well.

"Insomnia and an awful case of the giggles," explained Fiona.

"Do you plan on having insomnia tomorrow or the rest of the week?" asked Principal Sterling.

"No way. My insomnia days are over."

"What about your giggle days?"

"Them too."

And then that was all. Principal Sterling said she could go.

Except for one thing. Fiona had to give a sincere apology to Mr. Bland. Fiona made a face at that but then said okay. She supposed it could have been worse. She got up to leave.

"Oh, Fiona," said Principal Sterling. "Before you go, could you tell me what was so funny? I could use a good laugh."

Fiona wasn't sure if what she thought was funny and what Principal Sterling thought was funny would be the same thing. But she had been pretty nice, and Fiona wanted to hear her laugh again. "Mr. Bland in tightie whities."

Principal Sterling smiled. "Thank you. You can go now."

Fiona nodded. She could hear the sounds of pennies splashing all the way down the hall.

On the walk home from school,

Fiona passed by Ordinary Fudgery and got a sick feeling in her stomach. In the window, right beside a sign that read EGGNOG AND PUMPKIN-PIE FUDGE ARE HERE! was a poster for *The Nutcracker*. Under the date, time, and how to buy tickets was a picture of Clara watching a toy soldier fight a rat. Her eyes were wide, and she looked afraid.

Fiona's own eyes grew wide as she stared at the poster. She pictured a train barreling straight for her, getting closer and closer every second, while she was lying there helpless on the tracks, tied up with heavy rope made from somebody's underwear. Unless she figured out a way to untie herself, she would be run over—smushed!—by *The Nutcracker* Express.

Fiona couldn't let that happen. She wanted to be on the train, not under it. This was her *one* chance to be a big-time ballerina. She had to figure out what to do. Operation Underwear had sort of worked. But not in the way that she'd thought it would. Sure, picturing Mr. Bland in his tightie whities made her laugh and sort of forget her nervousness. Sort of. But it made her laugh so much and so hard that she turned into a pile of giggle mush. And that was no good. What if that happened on the stage? It would be almost as bad as barfing on Benevolence. "What is the matter with that angel?" people would want to know.

Fiona pulled out her cell phone from her coat pocket. Mom answered on the fifth ring. "Hello, darling."

"Did you, I mean Scarlet, push Nash off the boat?"

"I did, and it was a big splash. The director said that we got it on the first take, but I had so much fun, I asked if I could do it again."

"And did he let you?" asked Fiona.

"Of course, darling."

"Were you nervous?"

"When?" said Mom.

"When you had to push him off the boat?"

"No, not nervous. Excited."

"Were you ever nervous?" asked Fiona. "Like when you were just starting, maybe?"

"Only once, when I ate an egg salad sandwich with expired mayonnaise. Why?"

"Just wondering," said Fiona.

One evening after dinner, Fiona plopped down on the couch beside Mrs. Miltenberger. Max was on the floor cleaning his goggles with the corner of his cape.

"He's on!" Mrs. Miltenberger pointed the remote

control at the TV and turned up the sound. Dad had been giving the weather report on TV for more than a week now, but it still was exciting.

Fiona got up from the couch and stood next to the TV. As she watched her dad on the screen, she moved her arms from left to right, just like he did.

"With this high pressure area to our west combined with cold temperatures, we have just about the right ingredients for some snowfall," Dad said.

Fiona took it from there. "Do you see all this white stuff over there?" she said, pointing to a pretend map behind her. "That's a snowstorm. And it's headed right for us over here." She jabbed the air with her finger to show where Ordinary would be on the map.

Fiona grinned at Max, who had put down his goggles and was staring at the invisible map behind her. Mrs. Miltenberger laughed. "Very good, Fiona. What else?"

"You know how you need ingredients to make a cake?" Fiona continued. "Well, you need ingredients to make snow, too. You need clouds, a gray sky, cold wind, and a couple of ice cubes. Mix that all together and bake it at below-freezing temperature until flakes start falling." Fiona twirled. "And that's how you make snow. Oh, and since I don't have a math test tomorrow, I predict that we'll get a foot of it. Because for some reason, it never, ever snows when I have a math test. This has been 'Fiona's Fabulous Forecast.' Back to you, Baxter."

Mrs. Miltenberger clapped and laughed. "Bravo!"

Max jumped up and shouted, "All right, no school tomorrow!"

Fiona curtsied. She wished for a foot of snow so she could have a day without Mr. Bland. She had said she was sorry to him, just like Principal Sterling told her to do. But after that, Mr. Bland gave Fiona the awful job of Classroom Courier. Even though it was her turn to be Electrician.

Max leaped onto the couch and practically landed in Mrs. Miltenberger's lap. "Can I stay up late?" he asked. "Please!"

"No, sir, you cannot." She patted his head and adjusted his cape, which had swung around to the side.

"Can I?" asked Fiona, hoping the fact that she was nine years old might finally pay off in some way. Mrs. Miltenberger shook her head.

"But Fiona and Dad said it's going to snow," Max said.

"You know how crafty the weather can be," said Mrs. Miltenberger. "Besides, I've got big plans tonight to catch up on *Heartaches and Diamonds*. It was my turn to drive the Bingo Bus this week, so I had to record the last four episodes. I think Nash Barrington's evil twin, Marcus, is about to wake up from his coma."

"That stinks," said Max.

"Stinks?" said Mrs. Miltenberger. "If Marcus

wakes up soon, he'll take over as chief of staff of Sparkling Valley Hospital, and then everybody's doomed."

"Can I watch too?" asked Fiona. It had been a long time since she'd watched an episode of her mom's show. These days, she saw more of her mom on TV than in real life. Her mom had gone from a starring role in Fiona's life to one of those extras who didn't have a big part.

"Not tonight, dear," said Mrs. Miltenberger. "Your father would not be very happy to know that I let you stay up past your bedtime on a school night."

"But if it snows, we won't have school tomorrow," reasoned Fiona. "And then it's not really a school night."

"Yeah," said Max, his arms folded across his chest.

Mrs. Miltenberger gave Fiona and Max a look out of the corner of her eye, which Fiona took to mean Nice Try.

"Can I watch tomorrow then?" Fiona asked.

"If you don't have school tomorrow, then, yes. Now run upstairs, get your pajamas on, and get settled," said Mrs. Miltenberger. "I'll be up to tell you good night in a bit."

Max got to his feet and raced past Fiona to the stairs. Fiona stayed behind. She wasn't ready for sleep just yet. "Did you see Nash get pushed off the boat?"

"No. When did that happen? Wait . . . don't tell me. You'll ruin the surprise." She shook her head. "Pushed off a boat, huh?"

Fiona nodded.

"Scarlet, right?"

Fiona nodded again. "Who else?"

Mrs. Miltenberger clapped her hands. "I knew it. I knew something would happen to keep them from getting married. Nash deserves so much better. Scarlet is up to her usual tricks again."

"Like posing as a nurse and trying to poison her sister?" asked Fiona.

"That's right. Then she lied in court to make it look like somebody else did it, and then she faked a car crash so she could claim she had amnesia."

"She sure is busy," said Fiona. Of course, TV problems were worse than real-life problems. Sometimes.

"She's a slippery noodle, that one. Somehow, she always seems to find a way out of it," said Mrs. Miltenberger. "She knows how to get out of any sticky situation."

Fiona wished that Scarlet von Tussle could help Fiona out of her own sticky situation. To someone like Scarlet, getting rid of stage fright would be small potatoes compared to murder and faking amnesia. And then she began to wonder, *What would Scarlet do?*

She went to the phone in the kitchen and dialed

California again. Ten rings and her mom's voice on the recorded answering message. Why wasn't she answering? Fiona scratched her cheek. After a long beep, she left the following message:

"Mom! I need your help, pronto. Call me back right away. I have to ask you something very important. Oh, yeah, this is Fiona. Your daughter." She banged down the phone. Of all the moms in the world, why did hers have to live in California? She might as well live on Mars.

• Chapter 6 •

The next morning, there was no snow and no message.

After school, Fiona sat on the bench in the dressing area of La Petite and tugged at her leg warmers. She pulled them up so they covered her knees and then scrunched them down toward her ankles. Up, down, up, down, she fiddled with them as she watched girls from her class trickle in through the front door.

As Fiona sat pulling and twisting, her brain was

stuck in California. The same place it had been all day.

The door to La Petite swung open again, and blasts of winter air stung her face. Definitely not California! She shivered and walked down the hall out of the way of the cold.

Fiona warmed her *derrière* by the radiator and looked at the framed photographs that lined the hall. She stopped right in front of her favorite.

The ballerina in the picture stood on the tips of her toes with her arms above her head in the shape of an *O*. Her costume was beautiful like all of the others. But there was something about her face that Fiona had always really liked. She was smiling, but not a full smile exactly. An almost smile. A knowing smile. Like she had a secret.

But today, for some reason, Fiona didn't very much appreciate that secrety, knowing smile. In fact, it made her grit her teeth. "You don't know what it's like," Fiona said to the ballerina in the picture.

Voices rose excitedly from the practice room—shrieky voices. Above them, she heard Madame Vallée.

Fiona raced down the hall, through the dressing area, and into the practice room to see what was going on. There she found Madame Vallée surrounded by a crowd of squealing girls. Fiona spotted Cleo. "What is it?"

"Madame Vallée has a surprise for us!" said Cleo, hopping about excitedly.

Fiona grabbed Cleo's hand and slid into the spot beside her.

"Now, ladies," said Madame Vallée, holding up a box, "today we begin to learn the dance of the Nutcracker angels. But before we do, I have a special treat for you. Would you like to see your costumes?"

Everyone cheered, "Yes! Yes!" Even Fiona's heart felt a little lighter. She loved to look at the beautiful costumes Madame Vallée chose for recitals. Almost as much as she loved learning the dances. Even if she would never wear one onstage, looking at them was absolutely delicious. And that was a flat-out fact.

Madame Vallée lifted the lid and tossed it onto the floor. The room fell quiet. Fiona kept her eyes on Madame Vallée's hands. They slowly began to unfold the tissue paper inside the open box.

Fiona's mouth watered. She swallowed and leaned forward, trying to get a better look.

Then, with one whip of her arm, Madame Vallée pulled the costume from the box. Everyone gasped.

Fiona's knees wobbled, and she almost forgot to breathe. The most sparkling costume in the history of all La Petite costumes was right there in front of her. But it was more than that. It was a big-time ballerina costume. Just as beautiful as the ones in the pictures hanging in the hallway.

It was bright white and trimmed with sprays

of delicate gold ribbon. The skirt, a full tutu, with layers upon layers of lace, sloped like a perfect golden waterfall. And peeking out from the sides was a pair of feathery wings. Fiona had never seen anything like it. It dazzled like a night star.

"What do you think?" asked Madame Vallée, twirling the beautiful thing. "*Ooh-la-la*, beautiful, yes?"

Fiona nodded. It was *ooh-la-la* beautiful, and her eyes were glued to it.

As Madame Vallée gently tucked the costume back into its box, Fiona imagined herself as a Nutcracker angel. Spinning, leaping, twirling. And at that moment, she realized that she had never wanted anything more.

Madame Vallée looked from one girl to the next. "Now, I have announcement to make, so please open your *oreilles* and listen. The dance of the Nutcracker angels has a part for a *prima* angel. One who shows the angels the way, leading the dance."

Everybody seemed to hold their breath, waiting for Madame Vallée to continue.

"I have posted a sign-up sheet on the Brag Board. If you are interested, write your name. But, before you do," she went on, "you should know that the lead angel must show commitment and dedication." She looked right at Fiona. "And she must show up for every practice *and* the performance."

Fiona cringed.

"I will announce the *prima* angel next week," said Madame Vallée, looking pleased with herself.

Right after practice was over, a line formed from the Brag Board and wound all the way down the hall. It seemed as though everybody wanted to be the *prima* angel. Cleo and Fiona stood at the back of the line watching as the girls ahead of them took turns printing their names on the sign-up sheet.

Fiona heard the Three Bees buzzing around her. "I thought it was supposed to snow today," said Beatrice.

"Yeah," said Benevolence. "Did you ever notice how dumb weather people are never right?"

"Yeah, never," Bonnie chimed in.

Fiona clenched her hands into fists. She turned

on her heels to face the Three Bees. "They aren't weather people," she said. "They are meteorologists. And they aren't dumb!"

They stared at her. Even Benevolence was speechless.

"Duh!" said Cleo, in loyal support.

Fiona turned back. The line inched forward.

Then, from behind Fiona, Benevolence piped up. "I don't know what you're doing in line, Vomit-stein."

That was the cue for Beatrice and Bonnie, because they both started making awful gagging noises. Benevolence kept on going. "We all know you won't show up to dance in *The Nutcracker* anyway. So what's the point in signing up for the lead part?"

"Buzz off!" said Cleo, cracking her knuckles.

The Three Bees shook their heads and pushed past them to the front of the line.

"I wish one of us would get the part of the *prima*

angel," said Cleo. "That would send Benevolence Castle to the moon."

"You would make a good *prima* angel," said Fiona.

Cleo shrugged. "I'd be okay. I just want to see the look on Benevolence's face when Madame Vallée calls my name . . . or yours."

Fiona hung her head.

"How's it going with Operation Underwear?" said Cleo.

"It's not working right," she said. Fiona watched as the Three Bees shoved one another to be the first to write their names on the sheet. "I mean, it made me forget about my nervousness. But how am I supposed to dance in *The Nutcracker* with a case of giggles?"

Cleo bit her lip and squinted her eyes like she was concentrating. "But what if Mr. Bland in his underpants just happens to be the funniest thing in the universe? And that's why you laughed. I mean,

I can't think of anything funnier. Can you?"

Fiona shook her head. "Definitely not."

"What if you tried Operation Underwear in front of people who aren't Mr. Bland. You know, strangers, a bunch of them—an audience! Maybe that wouldn't be so hilarious."

Fiona thought about this. And then she smiled. It was a secrety knowing smile.

"What?" asked Cleo cautiously.

Fiona grabbed Cleo's hand and marched right up to the sign-up sheet on the Brag Board. Fiona picked up the pen and wrote *Fiona Finkelstein* in big letters.

"I have a favor to ask you," she said.

∘ Chapter 7 ∘

Asking your best friend for help can sometimes mean big trouble. That's what Fiona realized when Cleo showed up at her house first thing Saturday morning. She was armed with their new plan for Operation Underwear.

"What are those?" asked Fiona, pointing to the bright orange sheets of paper in Cleo's hands.

Cleo smiled and wiggled her eyebrows. She held up the flyers so Fiona could see. Large block letters in Cleo's messy handwriting filled the paper:

Fiona gasped. "I thought it was just going to be for the lunch bunch," said Fiona. "What are these for?"

"I figured if we're going to do this, we might as well do it big-time," said Cleo. "So, we've got to, you know, advertise." She patted her backpack. "I've got tape, scissors, and . . . oh yeah, I brought music and plastic bags."

"I think I'm going to be sick," Fiona said.

"Then it's a good thing I brought the bags."

Fiona looked at the flyers. "And why did you put *this* on there?" Fiona pointed to the part about her mom.

"Well, your mom is sort of famous. And my mom and dad can use more customers." Cleo set her backpack on the floor and sat down on the couch. "Did you decide what dance you're going to do?"

"The cancan?"

Cleo clapped. "That's just what I hoped you

were going to do! You're so good at the leg-kicking part. Where's your costume?"

"I'm not wearing a costume," said Fiona.

"What do you mean? You have to!" Cleo hopped off the couch and headed up the stairs to Fiona's room.

"My cancan costume is too small," said Fiona, following right behind. "It doesn't fit anymore."

Cleo disappeared deep inside Fiona's messy closet. After a few minutes, she reappeared with the pink and green cancan outfit in her hands. "Here you go," she said.

Fiona cringed when she saw the costume. She hadn't looked at it since that *one* recital. "It's not going to fit, I'm telling you."

"Just try," said Cleo, shoving the frilly costume at her.

A few yanks, tugs, twists, and stuffs later, Fiona was mostly in. Cleo couldn't get the back zippered all the way. But it fit so tight all over that there was no chance it would fall off.

"See, I told you," said Cleo, smiling. "It fits."

"If I breathe, the seams are going to burst," said Fiona.

"That's an easy one," replied Cleo. "Don't breathe."

While Fiona looked at herself in the mirror, Cleo put on the finishing touches—a pink, beaded headband, and green gloves that reached halfway up her arms. "There," she said. "Now, let's go."

Cleo grabbed Fiona's hand and pulled her downstairs and out the door, only stopping for her winter coat and boots.

Fiona wanted to turn back the moment she stepped outside. "I've changed my mind," she said. "I don't want to be the *prima* angel. I don't even want to be in *The Nutcracker*."

Cleo put her hands on her hips and frowned. "Fiona Finkelstein, I don't believe you."

"It's true," Fiona said, staring at her feet.

"No, it isn't. Besides, you can't back out now." Cleo held up the orange flyers. "What would I do with these?"

"Throw them away," said Fiona. That seemed like a no-brainer.

"But these are only half of them." Cleo grinned. "The rest I already put up."

• Chapter 8 •

After Fiona and Cleo got through
with it, the town of Ordinary looked
anything but ordinary. Even the
town's Christmas ornaments, wreaths, and ribbons
could not compete with Fiona and Cleo's bright
orange posters.

Fiona Flyers peppered every telephone pole,
parking meter, and storefront window. Even the
tree in the middle of Baker's Square was ablaze
with orange color.

As they got closer to Button's Family Restaurant,

Fiona saw a crowd of people waiting outside. Each one was holding a piece of bright orange paper. She couldn't believe her eyes.

"Wow!" said Cleo.

Fiona felt a wave of panic splash her in the face. She stopped in her tracks. "Come on!" yelled Cleo, tugging on her coat sleeve. But Fiona didn't budge. It was impossible to imagine all of those bundled-up people in underwear. Cleo got behind her. Fiona felt a push, and her legs started moving again. Cleo was steering her toward the crowd. "Excuse me, excuse me, move please," she said, pushing Fiona around the swarm of people and through the front door.

Inside, Button's Family Restaurant was bustling. The dining room was filled with noisy lunchtime chatter. Dishes clinked and clanked. Trays of food whizzed by in every direction.

Fiona stood wide-eyed in the middle of the restaurant. Except for one, every chair at every table was filled. People were crammed into booths and piled on top of one another at the counter.

"It's just like they say on TV," said Cleo. "It pays to advertise."

Fiona shook her head. "Let's go home."

"No way," said Cleo. "They're here to see you."

"I know."

Cleo pointed to the salad bar. "Go stand over there, and I'll get things going."

"I can't."

"It's called the cancan. Not the can't-can't."

Fiona looked around the room at all of the strange faces. None of them were looking at her. They were busy eating their lunch and talking. This was her best chance. Maybe most of them wouldn't even know she was there. Maybe she could go unnoticed. A couple of leg kicks, and then she could go home.

She breathed in slowly, careful not to burst out of her costume, and then nodded. Cleo grinned and made her way across the room.

Fiona slowly took off her coat and boots. She slipped on her ballet shoes and stepped toward the salad bar. She repeated to herself, *Don't go nutty, don't go nutty, don't go . . .*

"Is this thing on?" Cleo's voice came loud and clear through the speakers on the walls. She was standing by the cash register, tapping and blowing at the microphone.

The whole restaurant got quiet. Everyone looked in her direction. "Oh, good," she said. "Ladies and gentlemen, thank you for coming! And get ready for something amazing, incredible, and absolutely fantastical!"

Fiona felt the familiar tornado twisting in her stomach. *Don't go nutty,* she repeated. She put her hand on the counter to steady herself. She started with the couple sitting at the table closest to her. They were old, wrinkly, and as skinny as strings of spaghetti.

She began to imagine: boxer shorts with poodles

on them. Or, maybe tiger stripes instead. No, definitely poodles. And a matching T-shirt. And for the woman, granny panties—ones that were held up by elastic suspenders. She was glad she didn't live in the olden days if people had to wear underwear like that!

Lively music interrupted her underwear concentration. She saw Cleo positioning a CD player on the stand in front of the microphone. Fiona looked at the speaker on the wall above her when it came to life with music—what Madame Vallée called "The Gallop."

"And now," continued Cleo over the music, "presenting Fiona Finkelstein live onstage . . . or, well, I mean live over there by the lettuce." She pointed in Fiona's direction. And just as she did, every person in the whole restaurant shifted their gaze from Cleo to her.

A few people clapped.

Then they stopped. And they waited.

And waited.

And waited for Fiona to do something.

Anything.

And then, the door swung open, and in walked Baxter Buckworth.

○ Chapter 9 ○

Baxter Buckworth strode in, his toothy smile flashing as bright as a toothpaste commercial. He pulled out a chair at the only empty table in the restaurant. It was just two tables away from where Fiona stood. As he sat down, he picked up the plastic RESERVED sign from the middle of the table and laid it on its side. Then, he shook his napkin open, laid it across his lap, and looked around the room. His eyes stopped on Fiona.

Fiona's nerves rumbled deep in her stomach.

She swallowed hard and looked down at the floor. It was the only place in the restaurant without eyes staring back at her.

She stared at the sea of black-and-white checkered tiles beneath her feet. She shifted so that her ballet shoes fit inside one white square. *If only I could shrink into that tiny space in the floor.*

But Fiona knew she couldn't shrink. And she couldn't look at the floor forever either. So she had better get on with it. The music awaited!

She got back to underwear and the skinny spaghetti couple. Once their underwear was clear in her mind, she moved on to the next table, where a man and a woman sat in matching workout clothes. She imagined sporty ones with tennis rackets on them, because these two looked like they had just come from the court.

Fiona must have been thinking about their underwear for a long time, because all of a sudden she was distracted by the sounds of cranky voices filling her ears.

"What is she going to do?"

"Are you sure she's the daughter of that actress?"

"If I wanted to watch somebody do nothing, I would have stayed home and stared at my husband."

Fiona glanced over at Baxter Buckworth. He was talking to the waitress and pointing at his menu. At least he wasn't looking at her.

Then Fiona heard someone clear her throat from the other side of the room. It was Cleo. She saw Cleo's mouth form a word. Cleo said it without uttering a sound, but it might as well have been a scream. "Go!" She was saying. "Go-go-go!"

Fiona's brain had turned to bologna. She had already forgotten what kind of underwear she'd pictured. And now there was no time to start all over again.

So, she did the only thing she could think of.

Right leg. Up. And kick. Left leg. Up. And kick. She couldn't tell if her legs were straight, if her knees were high enough, or even if her toes were pointed.

Right leg. Up. And kick. Left leg. Up. And kick.

The restaurant chatter got louder. Fiona could hear mutters and murmurs from around the room. As they got louder, Fiona's leg kicks got higher, faster, and wilder.

She was doing it! She wasn't sure how she looked or if anybody was watching her. But that didn't matter. She was dancing! In front of people!

With each kick, she felt like she was kicking away a chunk of her worries and sending it straight to the moon.

I Can-Can! I Can-Can!

She looked at Cleo. Her big smile and wide eyes said it all: *Hello*, big-time ballerina!

And kick. And kick. And turn. And kick. And . . .

CRASH!

Fiona heard it before she felt it.

Her leg. Her wild, kicking, cancan of a leg knocked a tray of food out of a waiter's hand and sent it flying. Fiona fell backward. She landed with a thud, right on her *derrière*, at the feet of

the skinny spaghetti couple. And as she hit the floor, she saw a downpour of turkey with gravy, green beans, and a side of coleslaw splatter right on Baxter Buckworth's head. A direct hit. He was completely and totally soaked with today's lunch special.

● Chapter 10 ●

On the **walk** home from Button's Family Restaurant, Fiona tore down and crumpled every orange flyer she saw. She didn't want to leave a trace of this terrible day behind. She stuffed the crumpled flyers inside her coat so she wouldn't have to look at them.

When she found a trash can at Baker's Square, she shook them out of her coat. She gave one last glance at the bright orange pile and made out the words "amazing" and "fantastical" among the crinkled paper. She tried to think of words that were the opposite of "amazing" and "fantastical." But the only one she could come up with was something Scarlet von Tussle would say: "dreadful."

Baxter Buckworth would definitely agree. After he got basted with the turkey-gravy lunch special, after Mr. and Mrs. Button mopped him up, and after Fiona limped over to him to squeak out a "Geez, sorry," Baxter Buckworth wiped the gravy from his eyes, licked his fingers, and said, "Needs more salt."

Huh?

Fiona had braced herself for the arrival of Hurricane Baxter. But the storm never came. There was no howling or face color changing. Baxter Buckworth just took a sip from his water glass and then stood up to leave. "I'd better change before someone mistakes me for dinner," he had announced, calm as can be. Like he was used to having gravy dripping from his ears.

Had she gotten him all wrong before? Maybe he wasn't so bad after all. But just then, on his way out the door, he threw Fiona an over-the-shoulder Doom Scowl.

He thought she was dreadful, without a doubt.

As she headed home, Fiona kicked a pebble down the sidewalk. With each kick, she thought about her new troubles. Who would have thought that a couple of leg kicks could cause so many problems? She made a list of them in her head:

1. Caused turkey-gravy disaster on top of Baxter Buckworth's head

2. Got in big trouble with Cleo's mom and dad because of #1

3. Got Cleo in bigger trouble

4. Made Cleo mad because of #3

When she got to the last one, she stopped. Stage fright wasn't on the list! Her tornado-bellied stage fright was gone, gone, gone. No more Fiona Vomitstein, no more brain suckers. She had been saved—thank you, skinny spaghetti couple!—by underwear.

But now that her stage fright was gone, she realized she had a different problem. An even bigger one. She wasn't a big-time ballerina, she was a big-time disasterina. If she danced in *The Nutcracker*, who knew what could happen? The whole theater could catch fire!

She added this to the list in her head:

5. Will cause major disaster if I dance in
The Nutcracker

Fiona continued home. She kicked the pebble so hard that it hit an old lady in the knee. "Sorry!"

Big-time disasterina was right. What bad thing was going to happen next? Would Baxter Buckworth get mad at Dad for something that *she* had done?

Fiona quickened her pace, trying to get home before the news, or worse, Mr. Buckworth, reached her dad. She made her legs go faster and faster and sprinted into a full run when she turned down Marigold Street.

When she reached her house, she rounded the light post and raced up the brick front steps. "Dad!" she called as she burst into the living room.

Max was lying facedown across the coffee table, tracing his head onto a piece of paper. "He's in there." With a blue crayon he pointed to the kitchen without lifting his head.

"Dad?" She pushed open the kitchen door. Dad was sitting at the table, his head resting wearily on his arms. Uh-oh. She sank into the chair across from him.

"Hi, Bean."

"Hi," said Fiona. She stared at him, trying to figure out if she was in trouble or not. Sometimes it was hard to tell. His eyes looked tired, but the rest of his face looked pretty normal, and not all scrunched up and tight like it did when he was mad.

"Is there something you want to say?" he asked.

"No," said Fiona. "Is there something *you* want to say?"

He gave a half-smile and then his eyebrows twitched. The half-smile could mean he was happy, but could also mean he was annoyed. Half-smiles were the worst when you were trying to mood-read. And the twitching eyebrows didn't help.

Did he already know what happened? Was he waiting for a confession? She wouldn't be tricked into giving one, that's for sure. That's what always happened with the bad guys on those TV detective shows.

"Did you have a nice day?" he asked. Fiona observed: face normal, eyebrows twitchless. He wasn't giving anything away either.

"Did *you* have a nice day?"

"Fiona."

"Dad."

"Stop it!" he said. Face tight and scrunchy. Voice loud. Definitely mad.

"Okay, you've got me," Fiona said, unable to take it any longer. Her confession came out in a flurry. "It was an accident. A real, true, honest-to-goodness accident. It was the only way to see

if Operation Underwear worked. And it did work. But now there is something else wrong. And now I don't know how I'm going to be a big-time ballerina in *The Nutcracker* because who knows what terrible thing will happen? I mean, somebody could get hurt!"

She took a breath, but then the words kept coming. "And I didn't mean for Mr. Buckworth to get all splattered and his suit turkey-ed up. But if you ask me, he could use a new suit because he wears that same one all the time on TV and—"

"Bean," Dad interrupted, "I'm sorry, what are you talking about?"

"You don't know?" she asked.

"Know what?"

"Oh, thank you," said Fiona. She put her head down on the table in relief. "I mean, nothing. Definitely nothing. I was just mixed up about something. Forget I said anything." Finally, something had gone her way.

They sat quietly. And then she wondered why her dad wasn't saying anything. "What's the matter?" she asked, lifting her head. Now that she wasn't in trouble, it was safe to ask.

He gave her a smile. A phony one. "Oh, nothing for you to worry about, Bean." He mussed her hair and then got up from the table. "Mom called a little while ago."

"Did she get my message?"

"I don't know," said Dad. "She didn't say."

"I guess it doesn't matter now, anyway," said Fiona, scratching her cheek. "What did she say?"

"She was getting on a plane. Scarlet and Nash are getting married again, and they are shooting a honeymoon scene in Bermuda next week. She said she would call again later."

"Last week she pushed him off a boat, and this week they are getting married. Don't tell Mrs. Miltenberger," said Fiona. "She went through a whole box of tissues last time they got married."

"Right. Don't tell Mrs. Miltenberger. Got it," said Dad.

"Will she be home after her honeymoon?" asked Fiona.

"Mrs. Miltenberger?"

"Very funny," said Fiona.

"Not right away," he said. His back was to her as he rinsed the breakfast plates.

"Oh. Don't you wish Mom didn't live in California?"

He sighed and said, "I wish California and Ordinary weren't so far apart." He looked over his shoulder at Fiona and smiled, another phony one. "Now, who wants lunch? I can whip up some turkey sandwiches."

Fiona groaned.

Chapter 11

G ot your money?" asked Mrs. Miltenberger from the driver's seat of the Bingo Bus, which was really more like a minivan, painted orange.

In the backseat, Fiona squeezed a folded envelope in her coat pocket. "Ten dollars and twenty-nine cents. My whole life's savings."

"I've got twenty-five dollars in my piggy bank," said Max. "I'm rich!"

Fiona ignored him and asked, "Why does dry

cleaning cost so much if they don't even use water?"

Mrs. Miltenberger laughed. "That's a good question."

"What's the answer?" asked Fiona.

"I don't know. I suppose we'll have to ask a dry cleaner." Mrs. Miltenberger stopped the car in front of Button's Family Restaurant. "But until we do that, do not say anything to the Buttons about how much Baxter Buckworth's suit costs to clean, please. After what happened yesterday, I think you are very lucky they aren't making you empty the grease trap or scrub floors."

Fiona wondered why anyone would want to trap grease, but decided not to ask. She unbuckled her seat belt and opened the car door. She sighed and put a little moan right at the end, hoping that she wouldn't have to do this alone.

"We'll wait here," said Mrs. Miltenberger, looking into the rearview mirror at Fiona. "And don't forget the lemon bars."

Fiona grabbed the baking dish covered with aluminum foil from between her feet and climbed out of the car into the cold. She walked slowly toward the front door of Button's Family Restaurant and looked back over her shoulder at the Bingo Bus before going inside.

The front part of the restaurant was empty, except for Cleo, who was sitting at a table wrapping silverware into napkins. "Hi," said Fiona, not knowing how to start.

Cleo looked up at Fiona for a moment and then continued wrapping.

Fiona pulled the envelope from her coat pocket and made her way to the table. "Here you go," she said, shaking the envelope so the coins jingled. "This is for Baxter Buckworth's cleaning bill." She laid the envelope down next to the stack of napkins. "There's ten dollars and twenty-nine cents in there. I'm supposed to say that if it's not enough to pay for cleaning his suit, then I can keep giving your mom and dad all of my allowance money until it is."

Cleo wrapped another fork, knife, and spoon in a napkin and laid it on the pile without saying anything.

"And this is for your mom and dad, and you." She slid the dish onto the table. "Lemon bars from Mrs. Miltenberger. She wouldn't even let me have one, if that helps."

Cleo looked up, finally. "It does," said Cleo.

"Does that mean you are talking to me now?" asked Fiona, hopeful.

"No."

"Oh." Fiona's shoulders sank. "Well, will you tell me when you are?"

Cleo shrugged. "Okay."

Fiona shifted her feet and waited. She watched Cleo wrap four more sets of silverware. Fiona hated the silent treatment. "I'm real sorry for what happened. I'll do anything to make it up to you. Just name it."

Cleo flicked the edge of the napkin pile with her finger. "Anything? You'll do anything I ask?"

Fiona was beginning to worry. She took a deep breath. "Yep," she said, finally. "I'll do anything you want if you'll talk to me again."

"Okay, then," said Cleo, holding out her pinkie finger. "Pinkie swear."

Fiona looked at Cleo and then at her finger. "Tell me what it is first."

"No way, that's not how it works," said Cleo.

"Fine, but . . ."

"Wait, before you answer, I have to tell you that by the ancient rules of the pinkie swear, you, Fiona Finkelstein, swear to do anything I say. And this swear can't be broken. Ever. No matter what," said Cleo.

"I know the rules, Cleo."

"Okay, then." Cleo raised her hand higher and repeated, "Pinkie swear."

Fiona huffed. And then, after a moment, she

hooked Cleo's pinkie finger with her own. "Pinkie swear," she said, squeezing it. "Now, what is it?"

Cleo grinned. "So, the thing you have to do, the thing that you *swore* to do . . ."

"What is it?"

". . . is show up at *The Nutcracker* and dance."

• Chapter 12 •

It was the longest ballet practice ever.

Fiona couldn't concentrate on her ballet steps. Her *pirouettes* and *chassés* were a wreck. But it wasn't just her feet that were all over the place. Fiona's mind was on the pinkie swear and *The Nutcracker* Express. She was so filled up with worry that she wondered how her feet moved at all.

Not only that, she was worried about Mr. Buckworth. She remembered that look he'd given her as he left the restaurant. He had the scariest Doom Scowl she had ever seen.

"Fiona. Attention!"

Fiona was so busy worrying, she hadn't noticed that Madame Vallée had already started leading the warm-up routines. Fiona made her way to her usual spot in the second row beside Cleo, squeezing past Benevolence. "This is an upchuck-free zone," Benevolence said, trying to block her.

There was a part deep inside Fiona that told her to grab her stomach and start making gagging noises at Benevolence. If Benevolence wanted her to be Fiona Vomitstein, she would flat out show her Fiona Vomitstein! But that part was a small part inside her. And *that* part was being overruled by a bigger part, which told her to just ignore her. Hard as it was, that is what Fiona did.

At the end of practice, Madame Vallée asked each girl to go through the steps they'd learned for *The Nutcracker*, one by one. "Ladies, form a line here," said Madame Vallée, pointing to the wall with the giant mirror that stretched from floor to ceiling. "No, no, straight like *flèche*, not straight like banana," she said.

Fiona joined the end of the line, behind Cleo. The Three Bees were at the front, as usual. And Benevolence was first.

Cleo grabbed Fiona's pinkie with her own. "I

just know that Madame Vallée is going to choose you to be the *prima* angel."

"Don't say that."

"Why not?"

"Because something bad will happen when I dance. And if I'm the *prima* angel, I don't even want to think about what will happen to all the other angels."

"What are you talking about?" asked Cleo. "Your stage fright is gone! What could happen?"

"*Everything* could happen," said Fiona. "I am a big-time disasterina. Look at what happened at the restaurant with gravy-on-the-head Buckworth."

"Okay, that was bad," said Cleo. "But it turned out all right. You didn't get in trouble. And my mom and dad aren't mad at you anymore. And, most of all, I'm not mad at you anymore. So besides a little turkey gravy mess, where's the disaster?"

Fiona hadn't thought about it like that before.

Maybe she was just looking at the dirty side of the penny. Maybe if she flipped it over and looked at the shiny side, she'd see that Cleo was right.

"All right, Benevolence," said Madame Vallée, starting the music, "let us see you as a *Nutcracker* angel."

Fiona watched as Benevolence spun across the floor. As much as she didn't want to admit it, Benevolence was good. When Benevolence got through the whole dance, she rejoined the line and stood behind Fiona. One by one each girl followed, *pirouetting* and leaping across the floor. Madame Vallée simply nodded when each one finished and said, "Next."

As she inched forward in line, Fiona was filled with excitement. If Cleo was right, then she really could dance. She would show Madame Vallée and the Three Bees—and herself!—just what kind of a big-time ballerina she could be.

Fiona watched Cleo twirl across the floor. Cleo forgot to do the *grand jeté* at the end, but other than that, she did fine.

Then, at last, it was Fiona's turn. She got in her ready position and watched for Madame Vallée's nod. She checked her feet. They felt as light and marshmallowy as ever. As she waited, Fiona heard a buzzing in her ear. "Vomitstein." Benevolence said it again. "Vomitstein." The other Bees joined in. "Vomitstein, Vomitstein, Vomitstein," they sang.

But this time, the stings were easier to ignore. Fiona was determined to *pirouette* faster, *jeté* higher, and *glissade* bigger.

Finally, Madame Vallée nodded. Fiona answered with a nod of her own and then exploded like a firecracker across the floor with ferocious twirls. Every step, spin, and leap practically burst out of her. Her feet were so light, she seemed to fly around the dance floor.

With just the *grand jeté* left, Fiona got ready for her big finish.

She ran full force across the floor and leaped into the air, stretching her legs into a split. It was while she was in midair that Fiona realized that things had gone big-time wrong. She must have run too far and too hard, because she was heading right for Madame Vallée. And there was no way to stop.

"EEOWEEEGH!" shrieked Madame Vallée.

Fiona landed squarely on Madame Vallée, knocking her to the floor.

After she untangled her legs, Fiona rolled off of Madame Vallée and got herself to her knees. "Are you all right?"

Madame Vallée rubbed the side of her nose and winced. "*Oui*. I'm fine."

The rest of the class huddled around. Fiona grabbed one of Madame Vallée's hands and Cleo grabbed the other. They pulled her to her feet and held on until she was steady. "*Merci*, girls. Perfectly fine now."

Fiona looked at Cleo and shook her head. Cleo looked like she didn't know what to say. "Sorry, Madame Vallée," said Fiona. "I didn't mean . . ."

"This is nothing, Fiona dear. A little bruise." Madame Vallée touched her face. "*Ouille!*"

Fiona couldn't believe what had happened. *Disasterina!* And she couldn't stop staring at the red mark on Madame Vallée's face, which was turning purple right before Fiona's eyes.

"Well, that's enough for today, I think," said Madame Vallée, smoothing out her skirt. "We'll continue next time." She turned toward the door.

A chorus from the huddlers interrupted. "Madame Vallée! Madame Vallée!" everyone shouted. "You're supposed to tell us about the lead angel!"

"Ah, *oui*. How could I forget?" She turned around again, and Fiona and Cleo grabbed her hands when she started to wobble. She cleared her throat and said, "For the part of the *prima* angel, I have chosen Benevolence Castle."

The Three Bees went wild with excitement. They buzzed and flitted around the room for a hundred thousand years. The rest of the class followed Madame Vallée into the dressing room. Fiona and Cleo stayed behind.

"Do you think she's going to be okay?"

"Yeah," said Cleo. "But why did you do it, Fiona?"

"What do you mean?"

"I would have bet my whole piggy bank that Madame Vallée was going to choose you for the *prima* angel," said Cleo. "And she would have if you hadn't messed up on purpose and landed on her."

Fiona's mouth fell open. "I didn't mess up on purpose. I didn't mean for that to happen."

"Right."

"I didn't!" In fact, Fiona couldn't believe she'd never thought of doing that. What a good idea it was. Except the part about clobbering Madame Vallée.

"Then what was that all about?" asked Cleo.

"Disasterina," said Fiona. "I told you something bad was going to happen if I danced. Now do you believe me?"

Cleo cracked her knuckles and then locked pinkies with Fiona. "You still have to dance in *The Nutcracker*."

Fiona winced. How could she dance after she'd almost killed Madame Vallée?

"Can you believe it's Benevolence?" said Cleo.

"Well, she was really good."

"But Benevolence Castle as the *prima* angel? *Prima* rat, maybe. But not *prima* angel!"

Fiona shook her head, watching them. And as she watched Bonnie and Beatrice hooting and squealing around the room, she noticed a strange look flash onto Benevolence's face. It was there and then gone. But Fiona knew that look. It was a look of fear.

Chapter 13

On the days leading up to *The Nutcracker*, there was a strange chill in the air. Like the edge of something about to happen.

The Finkelstein house was a kettle ready to boil. Fiona spent her time trying to figure out whether she could keep her pinkie-swear promise or not. She went back and forth in her head a gazillion times, but she still wasn't any closer to knowing what in the world she was going to do. That was the thing about thinking. You could do it a lot and still not get anywhere.

If she danced in *The Nutcracker*, she was flat-out certain that something terrible would happen. Like maybe instead of just Madame Vallée, she would take out all of the dancers onstage next time. Or maybe she'd twirl right off the stage and into the orchestra pit, killing the violin player.

If she didn't dance . . . No, a pinkie swear was serious business. She had never—not ever!—broken one before. In the olden days, when the pinkie swear was first invented, the person who broke the promise had to cut off her pinkie finger. And even though Fiona had one pinkie finger to spare and couldn't remember the last time she'd used either of them for anything special, Fiona wanted to keep *all* of her fingers, thank you very much.

If Fiona did break the pinkie swear and didn't dance in *The Nutcracker* . . . sure, she would escape the disaster onstage, but she'd have to face an even bigger one: She'd lose her best friend (not to mention her pinkie).

Dad spent most of the days and nights at the TV station, tracking a big snowstorm that was heading for Ordinary. But when he was home, he and Max argued nonstop about Captain Seahorse. "I can think of at least ten reasons why you shouldn't be wearing this costume to school," Dad said. "First, and the most important, it's winter, and you will catch a cold. Second, superheroes don't go to school. Third, your teacher is not happy about it. Fourth, other parents have been giving me looks. Fifth . . ."

But if there was one thing that Max was good at—besides swimming—it was pretending Dad was invisible. So Captain Seahorse stayed put.

Only Mrs. Miltenberger was acting like her regular self. She had said she didn't want to play the referee to Dad and Max, so instead, she spent all of her time in the kitchen. "There's nothing like iced pumpkin cookies to smooth over even the biggest disagreements," she said. "My mother swore that this recipe could cure toothaches, stomachaches, and heartaches, and could make even the sorriest man smile."

But no amount of Mrs. Miltenberger's cookies seemed to cure what was bothering Fiona, Dad, or Max.

The day before *The Nutcracker,* Fiona decided to call California by way of Bermuda. She picked up the phone in the living room and put it to her ear. Just as she was about to dial, she heard her dad's voice on the other end. And then she heard another voice that was all too familiar.

"I understand your point, Mr. Buckworth, but . . ."

"Listen, Norm, I've been anchoring the evening news for a long time," said Baxter Buckworth.

"And I've been at WORD even longer."

"Right, but . . . ," said Dad.

"And I like things done a certain way. I've come to expect it. Call it, high standards."

"Of course," said Dad.

"And I expect the people I work with to meet those standards. Do you understand what I'm saying?"

"Yes," said Dad.

"The ratings have been slipping, and 'Finkelstein's Fabulous Forecast' has been, shall I say, less than fabulous. Now, this snowstorm is just what we need to put us on top. I've got some ideas that I'll share at tomorrow's production meeting."

"About that meeting," said Dad. "Fiona's dancing in *The Nutcracker* at the Grande Metropolis tomorrow, and I was hoping I could miss the meeting so that I could see her perform."

"Don't make me regret your promotion, Norm," said Baxter Buckworth. "Although, I can see your dilemma. Your daughter's dancing is an experience not to be missed. Might I suggest that you bring a raincoat."

"Now listen . . . ," said Dad.

"I expect I'll see you at the station."

Fiona hung up. The disasters kept on coming. Dad was in trouble, and it was all her fault. Her dancing was making him miss the snowstorm, and it sounded like he could even lose his job. Mr. Buckworth didn't appreciate how hard Dad worked to give good weather forecasts, which happened to be right most of the time. She wished she could do something to help.

After a few minutes, Fiona picked up the phone again. Mom answered on the twelfth ring.

"Is the honeymoon over?"

"Fiona darling, hi. No, not yet. How are you?" said Mom. "Hold on a minute, would you? Baron, Nick wants to do the running-down-the-beach sequence again. Right, he wants more foam in the shot, so he's off to get dish detergent. Let me know when we're ready."

Fiona shook the phone back and forth and banged it twice against her hand like she did when her super-sleuth detective flashlight wasn't working right.

"I'm back. Sorry about that. So, how are things? Dad tells me that you're going to be in *The Nutcracker*."

"Maybe."

"And that you're an angel," said Mom. "I didn't even know that there were angels in *The Nutcracker*."

"Yeah," said Fiona. "But . . ."

"I wish I could be there, but remind Mrs. M to bring the video camera so that I don't miss anything," said Mom.

"You're missing everything," said Fiona.

"What, Baron? Are you sure? That detergent can't be good for the fish. Oh, but that is a lot of foam, you're right. I'm coming."

· · 123 · ·

"Mom!" Fiona wished there were a way to dive into the phone and yank Mom back home so she could see what a real emergency was like.

"Gotta run, baby," said Mom. "Break a leg tomorrow. Kisses to Maxie and Mrs. M."

Fiona hung up in a huff. She went upstairs to her room to think. She passed Max on the stairs, kissed her fingertips, and then patted him on the head twice. "From your mother," she growled.

Fiona lay down on her bed and rubbed her forehead. She had too many things to think about. And they made her head feel like it was stuffed full of pebbles.

She yawned and pulled her blanket around her.

She closed her eyes and dreamt. Backstage at the theater, whispers were all around her. "Go, Fiona. Go, go. Now." Pointy fingers pushed at her until she stepped out from behind the dark curtain and onto the stage. Other dancers, all in costumes, all around her, were still as stone. She wove around them and found an empty place to stand in the shadow of a bear in a tutu.

The music started. The dancers moved, and Fiona tried to follow, but she didn't know the steps. Then, she felt something pulling at her feet. She looked down. Three rats were chewing at her marshmallow toes. She kicked at them and shook her feet, but they clamped their rotten teeth tighter and hung on. She leaped and spun, finally shaking off the first one, then the second, and at last the third. Once free, Fiona was ready to dance.

She *pirouetted* across the stage, making up steps as she went along. She tried to steer clear of the other dancers. And she did, at first. But then, her feet got away from her, and before she knew what was happening, she was a tornado blowing around the stage, knocking down every dancer and every person in the audience. Suddenly, Baxter Buckworth appeared onstage with a mighty Doom Scowl on his face and said, "Wait until I tell your father about this." But

Fiona couldn't stop. People screamed, "Look out!" and, "Stop her!" and, "It's Disasterina!"

"I can't stop!" yelled Fiona, and Baxter Buckworth's face grew wide with horror. "I can't!"

"I can't!" she yelled again, this time waking herself from the nightmare. She sat up in bed and threw off her blanket.

"You can't *what?*" asked Mrs. Miltenberger, at Fiona's bedroom door. "Are you feeling all right? Your face is all red." She touched Fiona's forehead and cheek with the back of her cool hand. "A little warm. But your engine always has run a little hotter than most."

"What's that?" Fiona's eyes grew wide when she saw what Mrs. Miltenberger was holding in her other hand.

"Mrs. Button picked this up from La Petite for you—wasn't that nice?" Mrs. Miltenberger turned *The Nutcracker* angel costume on its hanger. "Do you want to try it on?"

Fiona's heart thumped in her chest. The gold and white tutu sparkled before her eyes. She scratched her cheek. Of course, she really did want to try on that *ooh-la-la* beautiful costume.

Who wouldn't? But she was afraid that trying it on would make her want to dance even more. "No," she said, remembering the dream.

Mrs. Miltenberger lowered her eyebrows at Fiona. "No? Well, maybe later, then. I'll just hang it in your closet—"

"No!" said Fiona, louder than she expected. Mrs. Miltenberger stopped and waited for an explanation. "I mean," Fiona continued, "can you put it downstairs or someplace else for now? There's no room for it in my closet." She glanced at the rest of her room. "Or any place else in here." She looked from Mrs. Miltenberger to the costume and bit her lip.

"All right, then." Mrs. Miltenberger eyed the sprawling mess in Fiona's room and shook her head. "You know, you really should try to tidy up a bit, dear." Then she turned and left, taking *The Nutcracker* angel costume with her.

◦ Chapter 14 ◦

Before she could go to sleep that night, Fiona gazed out her bedroom window into the sky. So dark it was that she could see only her reflection in the glass and nothing else. Where were all the stars? She only needed one, after all. One to wish on. But the sky was empty.

Fiona growled. *Sneaky stars. Even they are against me.*

The next morning, Fiona poked her head out from underneath the thick bedcovers. She shivered from the cold. The gray light from the window told her it was morning and nudged her eyes open. She rubbed them and yawned. And then, as she turned over, she saw it.

She lay there frozen, her eyes wide with surprise.

Hanging on the back of her door was the beautiful angel costume. *Her* costume.

What was it doing here? Mrs. Miltenberger was supposed to have put it away downstairs, out of sight, someplace where Fiona couldn't see it. Fiona hadn't wanted to see the lace tutu with its golden sprays of ribbon that hung along its waist. She didn't want to see any part of it at all.

But now, here it was. Right in front of her. And it was so dazzling that she couldn't resist.

Fiona got out of bed, took a deep breath, and walked over to it. As she set her eyes on the costume's sparkling gold lace and fluffy wings, her heart began to thump. "Oh, my," she said softly.

She held the costume out from her and spun it

around, taking it all in. Up close, it was a gazillion times more wonderful.

Gently, she pulled the costume off the hanger and hugged it to her. Her heart thumped louder and faster. Holding it tight, Fiona whirled all around her room. Was she imagining it? Or were they the best whirls she had ever done?

Then, as fast as she could, Fiona slipped out of her pajamas and into the costume. As soon as she pulled the straps onto her shoulders, she set off, whirling again. This time, though, she was even faster.

She bounced up and down, lighter than a marshmallow, even lighter than a feather. Fiona didn't know how she was doing it, but she felt like she could twirl to the moon and show those stars, wherever they had been hiding, a thing or two.

She leaped over her caved-in dollhouse and then onto her bed. She jumped and twirled from one end of the bed to the other. Dancing around the piles of clothes and toys on the floor, she paused in the corner of her room and got ready for her *grande jeté*. She ran and kicked out her legs, shooting through the air and then landing perfectly near the door. Which opened before her.

"Good, you're up," Mrs. Miltenberger said. "We've got a busy, busy day ahead. Your father forgot his ticket for *The Nutcracker*, so we need to get to the station and drop it off, then drop off the cookies at Basket Bingo, and then get you downtown to the theater."

"I don't think Dad should come to *The Nutcracker*," said Fiona. "And you and Max probably shouldn't either."

"Why on earth would you say a thing like that?" asked Mrs. Miltenberger. "Of course we're coming. Everybody's coming. It's a sold-out performance! And your father wouldn't miss it for the world."

"But what if he gets in trouble for going?"

"In trouble with whom?"

"Baxter Buckworth."

"Oh, Fiona. This is your big day," said Mrs. Miltenberger, pinching Fiona's cheek. "You shouldn't worry so much."

That was easy for her to say. Mrs. Miltenberger wasn't the one in a tutu who was about to destroy the Grande Metropolis Theatre.

"Now get moving, because we've only got an hour. Can you be ready?" asked Mrs. Miltenberger.

Could she? That was the big question. She had made up her mind last night that she couldn't. Losing her best friend and a finger was one thing (or two things, really), but causing some huge disaster in front of lots of people was even bigger.

"Fiona, can you be ready?" Mrs. Miltenberger repeated.

But wait a second. There weren't any disasters just now. She had danced all over her bedroom and not one crash, trip, or fall. She hadn't hurt herself or anything else. No disaster or destruction of any kind. What was different? The costume?

Fiona imagined herself onstage at *The Nutcracker*. She imagined herself twirling and leaping. Could she do it without something awful happening?

She smiled cautiously. "Okay," she told Mrs. Miltenberger. "I think I can."

○ Chapter 15 ○

Ordinary's first snowflakes of the season began to fall as Mrs. Miltenberger, Fiona, and Max made their way to the TV station. As they drove across town, Fiona pressed her forehead to the cold window of the car and watched as the flakes began to cover the grass.

"Isn't this exciting?" said Mrs. Miltenberger. "Your father's forecast was right on target. He says we'll have ten inches by morning. Everybody's got their snow boots on—right, gang?"

"Right," said Fiona from the backseat.

Max, sitting next to her, raised his leg so that Mrs. Miltenberger could see his boot in the rear-view mirror. Part of his bare leg stuck out from under his long coat. "Right," he said.

"Max, you didn't!" yelled Mrs. Miltenberger as she swerved to the side of the road. She hit the brakes, and Max and Fiona lurched forward. Mrs. Miltenberger turned around in her seat. "Where are your pants? You were wearing them at the house. I saw you!"

Max shrugged.

"Unzip your coat, young man," she said.

As Max pulled down the zipper on his green winter coat, Mrs. Miltenberger shook her head. Fiona looked at the swim trunks and string of medals hanging down on Max's bare chest. She caught a glimpse of his cape stuffed behind him. "Uh-oh."

"Your father is going to kill me," said Mrs.

Miltenberger. She faced front again and rested her head on the steering wheel. "And we don't have time to go back home and change."

"Can't he just keep his coat on the whole time?" asked Fiona. "Then Dad won't see."

"Yes, that's what we'll have to do." Mrs. Miltenberger turned back around again. "Can you do that, Max?"

Max crossed his arms over his chest.

Mrs. Miltenberger sighed. "I mean, Captain Seahorse, can you keep your coat on during *The Nutcracker*?"

"Fiona's not wearing regular clothes," he said.

"That's because she's in the show," explained Mrs. Miltenberger. "You, little man, have a part in the audience, where people wear proper pants and shirts."

Fiona helped him zip his coat up all the way to the neck as Mrs. Miltenberger pulled away from the curb. "Fiona, when we get to the station, I'll wait in the car with the captain here, and you take in the cookies and your dad's ticket."

"Okay," said Fiona. Her nerves were starting up. A nervousness of what terrible thing awaited her. She wanted to get the whole thing over with. Because not knowing what was going to happen when she danced was like waiting for a monster to jump out of the closet.

Mrs. Miltenberger pulled into the WORD-TV parking lot and stopped the car. "Don't dillydally," said Mrs. Miltenberger. "We are short on time."

Fiona got out of the Bingo Bus and stepped into the powdery snow. She pushed it with the toe of her boot. Perfect for sledding, but not wet enough for a good snowball.

After grabbing Dad's ticket and the box of iced pumpkin cookies from the front seat, she went up the front steps of the TV station and inside. Down the hall, she counted the office doors on the left. When she got to number five, she went in and put down the box and ticket on the desk.

Voices from down the hall got her attention. She stood in the doorway and peered down the hall. Gabe Durand was talking to a tall lady with a clipboard. Fiona was about to ask Gabe if he had seen her dad, but then she heard words that made her stomach flip.

". . . Norm Finkelstein . . ."

". . . problem . . ."

". . . broken satellite . . ."

". . . no weather report . . ."

". . . who is going to tell . . ."

". . . Mr. Buckworth . . ."

You didn't have to be the smartest person on the planet to know that something bad had happened. Something that involved her dad and his weather report. And it was guaranteed to be something that Mr. Buckworth wouldn't like.

Fiona had to do something. She didn't want her dad to get into trouble again. But she wasn't sure what the problem was exactly. They started to walk down the hall away from her, so she followed them. She caught up to them inside the room with the cameras. "What's wrong?" Fiona asked.

Gabe looked surprised to see her. "Can we help you?" asked the lady with the clipboard.

"Fiona, your dad's not here," said Gabe. He bent down so that his face was on the same level as hers. "He's stuck halfway between here and Waggerville with a broken van and no live feed."

"What does that mean?" asked Fiona.

"It means that he can't do a live report on the weather from Waggerville or Piedmont or anywhere else." Gabe turned to the lady, pulled a quarter from his pocket, and said, "Let's flip for it. Heads I tell Buckworth, and tails you do."

The lady replied, "Why can't Henry fix the satellite receiver?"

"He's working on it," said Gabe. "The best Norm can do now is phone in his report on the weather conditions. But Mr. Buckworth isn't going to like that."

"Why not?" asked Fiona. That sounded like a perfectly acceptable thing to do.

They looked at her as if they were surprised that she was still standing there. "Because, this is the first major snowstorm of the season, and the chief meteorologist—your dad—is in the middle of Waggerville without a working camera, a map, or a computer. We've sent a truck to go get him, but he won't make it here in time. Other TV channels will be dazzling viewers with more snow reports than you can imagine. And what will we have? A guy on the phone."

"Can't somebody report on the weather from here?" Fiona asked.

"Who?" they asked. It was clear that neither of them wanted the job.

Fiona took a deep breath. She thought about how Mrs. Miltenberger had told her not to dillydally. She thought about how she was supposed to be on her way to *The Nutcracker* right now. She thought about her pinkie swear. She thought about all sorts of terrible things that might happen if she did something. And then she thought about how much trouble her dad might get in if she didn't.

She looked up at Gabe. Then she looked at the cameras, at the other news people shuffling about, and at the blue screen in the corner where her dad gives the weather report to a hundred thousand people.

Fiona swallowed hard. Her mouth was dry and felt like it was packed with cotton balls. Her heart had picked up its tempo.

A hundred thousand!

She took a deep breath. Then she unbuttoned her long winter coat and tossed it on the floor, revealing her *Nutcracker* angel costume. She looked at it and smiled triumphantly.

"Me," she told them. "I'll do it."

• Chapter 16 •

Maybe it was the gold sparkles of the costume that did it. Or maybe it was the flat-out fact that a fourth grader in a tutu reporting on the weather was better than a chief meteorologist talking about it on the phone. Or maybe it was because they had to go on the air in forty-five seconds, and there were no other ideas.

But whatever *their* reason was, Fiona was doing it to help her dad.

"You can't be serious," said the lady. She turned

to Gabe. "You can't put a ten-year-old on TV to report on the weather."

"I'm nine," said Fiona.

"Even better," said Gabe, pinning a microphone to the gold strap of her costume and smiling. "Okay, Fiona. Go ahead and stand in front of the blue screen."

Fiona took her place and stared into the lens of the large camera in front of her.

"Gabe, have you lost your mind?" asked the lady.

"Not entirely, Heidi." Gabe winked at Fiona and handed her the remote control that changed the maps. "And you remember how to use this, right?"

"Yep."

"What do you mean?" said Heidi.

"Fiona's an old pro," said Gabe. "Right, Fiona?

Fiona nodded.

"Wonderful. The first map is the total accumulation in our viewing area, and the second is . . ."

"Okay." She swallowed hard.

"Thirty seconds!" yelled somebody from behind the cameras.

Fiona's heart pounded. What was she doing? What was she thinking? Dancing in *The Nutcracker* was one thing. But TV, *live* TV, that was something flat-out altogether different.

"Twenty seconds!"

Fiona felt woozy. Her hands were sweaty. She wiped them on her lace tutu, but it didn't help. She tried to breathe, but she'd forgotten how. Had the brain suckers gotten to her already?

Her head started to spin. No, it wasn't her head. It was the room. The room was spinning all around her.

Gabe pointed to the TV beside the camera. "Remember to watch yourself here so you know what map is showing up behind you," he said.

"Ten seconds!" shouted someone else.

"Uuuhhh," Fiona moaned.

Do not go nutty, do not go nutty, do nut go nutty. . . .

"Five seconds!"

"And four . . ."

"And three . . ."

"And two . . ."

"And . . ." Gabe pointed to Fiona and said, "Go!"

That's exactly what Fiona wanted to do. She wanted to go far, far away. Australia, maybe. She wondered if a kangaroo's pouch might be available for rent.

But Fiona didn't go. She couldn't. She was frozen.

She thought she saw the camera operators and Gabe motioning to her with their arms, but she wasn't sure. Everything seemed to get fuzzy around the edges. Fiona shifted in her snow boots and looked all around her, trying to clear the fuzz. As she did, she saw something in the TV.

She leaned closer to get a better look. She blinked. Were her eyes playing a trick?

Fiona blinked her eyes again. She was amazed at what she saw. There on the TV was a ballerina from one of the pictures at La Petite. In her gold and white tutu, she looked as light and feathery as a stem of Queen Anne's lace. But even more than that, she looked ready to dance.

"Fiona," whispered Gabe, "do something, or we'll have to go to commercial!"

And then something clicked in her head. Fiona smiled. And the big-time ballerina smiled back. It was a secrety knowing smile.

"Good afternoon, Ordinary!" she said. "My name is Fiona Elise Finkelstein, and this is 'Finkelstein's Fabulous Forecast'!"

She twirled. "My dad, Chief Meteorologist Norm Finkelstein, is out there stuck in the snow. So until he gets here, I'm going to tell you about the weather today.

"Guess what? It's snowing outside!" She clicked

Accumu... 10"

NEWS 9 Finkelstein's Forcast

the button on the remote-control thingy and looked at herself in the TV. The map was behind her.

Whew.

"We've got four inches of snow already in Ordinary," she said. "And it says here that there are three inches of snow in Waggerville. Oh, poor Waggerville, you're an inch behind!

"And Piedmont and Pottertown, you've hardly got any at all. What's wrong with you, don't you like snow?"

She leaped to the far side of the blue screen and spun around. She clicked the button on the remote again. She was having fun now. "Let's talk temperatures. Brrrrr, it's only thirty-two degrees in Ordinary. That's freezing! Mrs. Miltenberger says that you should always wear a hat in cold weather because it keeps the warm air in your body from getting out through your ears. So, bundle up and wear a hat."

Fiona stood on her tiptoes and swirled her arms all over the map as she shouted temperatures from surrounding towns. "Thirty-four! Thirty-one! Thirty-six!"

As she was announcing the temperatures she heard some commotion at the back of the room.

But she kept on going. She was on a roll, and the weather couldn't wait. Besides, she was just about to do her big finish.

She *pirouetted* from one end of the blue screen to the other. When she came to a stop, she said, "And now, for the forecast. My dad says we are in for a whopper of a storm. I think it's going to snow for the rest of the day and into the nighttime. Ordinary will probably get about ten inches of snow by the time the storm blows through.

"But here's the really important stuff, so listen up. The snow is extra powdery, so it's good for sledding, but not as good for snowball battles. Or for making snow people. It needs to be wetter for that. But it's just flat-out perfect for my favorite thing to do in the snow—making snow angels."

Fiona smiled. "So, that's it for 'Finkelstein's Fabulous Forecast.' Have a fabulous snow day!"

And then she did her best curtsy for the camera.

"And we're out," said Gabe. He walked over to Fiona. "Well, that was really something."

"Fiona!" Max's voice came from the back of the room. Fiona looked past the bright lights above the cameras and into the darkness. She could make out Max's shape wriggling free from the clutch of a much bigger shape. Baxter Buckworth. "No fair," Max said, running over to her. "You got to be on TV!"

"I know, did you see?" Fiona said. She was having trouble believing it herself.

"Unfortunately, we did, along with a hundred thousand people in our viewing area," boomed Baxter Buckworth from behind Max. "Didn't I make it clear that this was not a day-care center? Who let her on the air?"

Fiona winced. Now she had done it. Her dancing had caused another problem. The monster in the closet was here, and his face was the color of pickled eggs.

"I did," said Gabe. "And I think she did a marvelous

job." His voice seemed to shake a little as he spoke.

"I agree two hundred percent," Mrs. Miltenberger chimed in. She stepped forward to give Fiona a hug. "I'm so proud of you." She kissed Fiona's forehead. "You really nailed it!"

"Mr. Buckworth," said Gabe, "think about it. Everybody loves kids." Baxter Buckworth cleared his throat. "Okay, well, maybe not everybody. But hear me out. While every other station is doing predictable, boring weather reports, *we're* doing the unpredictable. We've got kids. Costumes. Fun. Excitement. And . . ." Gabe looked at Fiona.

"Snow angels?" she said.

"That's right," continued Gabe, "we've got snow angels. Everybody will be talking about this. Our news will *be* the news. Think of the ratings!"

"Mr. Buckworth! Mr. Buckworth!" shouted a blond-haired lady as she ran into the room. She came to stop beside Mr. Buckworth and bent over at her waist, trying to catch her breath.

"What is it, Yolanda?"

She stood upright, but her breath was still coming hard and fast. "The phone . . . has been . . . ringing off the hook."

Buckworth winced. "I can just bet it has!"

Yolanda took a deep breath and pointed to Fiona. "Everybody loved that snow angel. They want to know . . . if she's going to be on every night."

Baxter Buckworth's eyebrows arched, and his puckered lips moved side to side like he was chewing on an idea. He looked at Fiona for a long time and then put his hand on Gabe's shoulder. "Let's talk more about this in my office." Gabe gave Fiona a wink and a smile.

"What's going on?" Dad said as he came into the room. His wet boots squeaked on the floor.

"Dad!" Fiona and Max rushed to his side.

"Norm," said Baxter Buckworth, "I want you to keep a close eye on that snow angel of yours."

"That *what* of mine?" Then Dad fixed his worried eyes on Fiona as if to say, *What have you done?*

But Baxter Buckworth flashed his toothy smile and laughed, which sounded a little like hiccups. Then, looking unsure of himself, he patted Fiona lightly on her head twice and gave Dad a slap on his back. "Good work, Finkelsteins."

• Chapter 17 •

I missed *The Nutcracker*," Fiona said when they got to Dad's office. The realization came over her so suddenly that it made her eyes prickle with tears.

Max lunged for Dad's desk chair, and Fiona let him have it. She wasn't in the mood to be chucked by Turner. Not after she had missed her chance to be a big-time ballerina AND had broken her pinkie swear with Cleo. She knew Cleo would never forgive her for this.

"Bean, with this storm, I'm betting that a lot of

people missed it." Dad picked up the phone on his desk, cradled it under his ear, and began flipping through the phone directory.

Fiona counted Max's spins. He fell off Turner after just five and barely missed Dad's trash can.

"Careful, Max," said Mrs. Miltenberger. "We'd have a hard time getting you to the hospital in this weather."

Max unzipped his coat, threw it on the floor, and mounted Turner once again. He flung his cape off to the side. Fiona and Mrs. Miltenberger looked at each other, and then at Dad. Still on the phone, his back was toward them.

"Good news, Bean," Dad said, hanging up and turning around. When he saw Max in his Captain Seahorse outfit, he froze.

"What's the good news?" asked Fiona.

Mrs. Miltenberger grabbed Max's coat from the floor and threw it around him. "Yes, tell us, we could use some good news about now."

Dad breathed out slowly and closed his eyes for a long second. When he opened them again, he said very slowly, "I just called the Grande Metropolis. *The Nutcracker* has been cancelled."

When they got home, there were nine messages on the answering machine. All of them were for Fiona. And all except for two were from Cleo.

Message #1: "Fiona, do you know you're on TV?"

Message #2: "Fiona, you are on TV in your *Nutcracker* costume!"

Message #3: "What are you doing on TV in your *Nutcracker* costume?"

Message #4: "Does your dad know you are doing this?"

Message #5: "Fiona, this is Madame Vallée. Tonight's performance of *The Nutcracker* has been postponed until next week because of the snow.

It's beautiful, no? Wait a second, I see that you are on the television. Look at you . . . I have said that you have the talent for the dance. But it looks also like you have the talent for the weather."

Message #6: "That was a great twirl!"

Message #7: "Fiona, this is Principal Sterling. I just wanted to say how much I enjoyed your weather report. I've never seen such enthusiasm for the weather. It makes me think we should start a meteorology club at school. See you Monday!"

Message #8: "Do you know how many people are watching you right now? A gazillion!"

Message #9: "Fiona, Madame Vallée just called, and *The Nutcracker* has been cancelled! It's been moved to next week. Call me when you're done with the weather!"

○ Epilogue ○

Fiona and Cleo said good-bye to Mr. and Mrs. Button and got out of the car in front of the Grande Metropolis Theatre. They walked up the stone steps hand in hand. Fiona's dad had taken her to a couple of plays here, but today was the first time Fiona really noticed how big the place was. And how *ooh-la-la* beautiful.

The floors of the lobby were covered in red carpeting that looked like velvet. Sparkly chandeliers, bigger than Fiona, hung in rows of three. Fiona stared up at them until she was dizzy.

"Listen," Fiona said, pulling on Cleo's arm. Music, real-live music with violins and flutes and trumpets, led them to the stage. The stage was much bigger than she'd remembered. Wider, too, as it stretched from one side of the theater to the other. A dark purple curtain hung from above was pulled back like wings.

Onstage, ballerinas dressed as toys, dolls, and soldiers stirred about. Fiona spied steps on the right side of the stage. "Come on," she told Cleo. "Over there."

As they made their way past the ballerinas on-stage, Fiona turned her head to look out into the audience. Hundreds of empty seats stared back at her. She felt a chill go through her. And she stopped.

"What?" asked Cleo, tugging on her finger.

Fiona wasn't sure what it was. She wasn't afraid exactly. She felt tingly. And thrilled.

"Ah, ladies, so very glad to see you," said Madame Vallée. "Isn't this superb?" The bruise on her face had faded into a purplish-yellow splotch.

Fiona nodded. She thought the excitement could burst out of her at any moment.

"Where do we go?" asked Fiona.

Madame Vallée pointed behind the stage to a narrow hallway. "Go that way to the dressing room. Some of the angels from your class are there already."

Fiona led the way down the tiny hall. It wound down and around tight corners, and just when Fiona thought they'd taken a wrong turn, she spotted a door with a sign that read DRESSING ROOM. She pushed it open and stepped into a noisy room.

Brightly colored costumes hung on metal racks just inside the door. Behind them, ballerinas in all shapes and sizes moved from mirror to mirror, putting on makeup and twisting their hair into tight buns.

Fiona spotted the Three Bees in the far corner of the room. Ugh.

"Hi, Cleo. Hi, Fiona," said Beatrice.

"Hi," Fiona and Cleo said at the same time.

"We saw you on TV," said Bonnie.

Fiona waited for Benevolence to say some kind of nasty thing about her TV performance. Or about being Fiona Vomitstein. Or about something else that was all kinds of mean. But she didn't say anything. Instead, Benevolence just stared at the floor.

Fiona and Cleo took off their coats and sat down beside the Three Bees.

"Are you okay, Benevolence?" asked Fiona.

Benevolence looked up at her quickly, and then back down at the floor.

"She's sick because she's scared . . . ow!" Beatrice said. She rubbed her arm from Benevolence's pinch.

"I am not scared," said Benevolence. "I have the flu or something."

"It *is* flu season," agreed Bonnie.

Benevolence got up and walked across the

room, disappearing behind a rack of costumes. Fiona followed and found her hiding between the Sugar Plum Fairy's skirt and a toy soldier's head. "Benevolence?"

"Go away."

Fiona squatted beside her. She spoke very gently. "Are you scared about being the *prima* angel?"

Benevolence's eyes flashed to Fiona's and then looked away. She poked her finger at the toy soldier's head.

"I think I can help," Fiona said, leaning in close to her. She whispered in her ear, "Have you ever heard of Operation Underwear?"

Benevolence looked at Fiona sideways, confused. Fiona explained everything. And when she was done, Benevolence had a smile on her face. It was a secrety-knowing smile. Fiona nodded, satisfied, and then rejoined the other angels. A few moments later, Benevolence returned, smiling still.

"Operation Underwear," Fiona said to Cleo.

Cleo nodded.

"Are you ready, angels?" asked Madame Vallée, coming into the dressing room. "We need to get your makeup and hair done. Benevolence, let's start with you."

After Fiona watched Beatrice and Bonnie trail behind Benevolence and Madame Vallée to the hair and makeup chair, Fiona spied her family at the door of the dressing room. She grabbed Cleo's hand and they both did *grande jetés* over to them.

"Let me see your legs," Dad said.

Fiona stuck one leg out in front of her, and then the other. Cleo did the same. "Okay, good," he said, giving Fiona's forehead a kiss. "Now go break one of them. You too, Cleo."

"Yeah, break one," said Max, hopping around on one foot and laughing.

He was wearing a blue sweater and green corduroys peeking out from under his coat.

"Hey, you've got clothes on!" said Fiona.

"Yep," said Max, smiling. "But I'm still Captain Seahorse all the time."

"What do you mean?" she asked.

"After an hour of negotiations, we figured out a way that he can still be Captain Seahorse and I won't be hauled in to Social Services," Dad explained.

Max pulled at the elastic waist of his pants and showed Fiona the seahorse swim trunks underneath. "See?"

"Anyway, we'd better go take our seats," Dad said. "We'll see you afterward. I thought we'd all go to Button's Family Restaurant for dinner." He grinned.

"Yeah," said Cleo, "my mom and dad said you're allowed back in as long as you promise not to dance."

Fiona smiled. That was a promise she was flat-out sure she could keep.

Acknowledgments

My Aunt Julie Over, the nice old lady in the hall (and the real Mrs. Miltenberger), deserves her very own golden tutu for a decade of hauling me back and forth to ballet class, always with a smile and with a Krackel bar in her pocketbook. Equally deserving is my mother, who for the record is not a thing like Fiona's mom (thank goodness), and who never, ever missed a recital.

Also tutu-worthy, for having read lots and

lots and lots of versions of this book—most of them admittedly dreadful—are the masters at Vermont College of Fine Arts, in particular, Kathi Appelt, Jane Kurtz, Uma Krishnaswami, Tim Wynne-Jones, Leda Schubert, and Margaret Bechard. A gazillion and a half thanks to the Revisionistas, aka Vermont Snow Angels: Gene, Gwenda, Micol, Lynda, and short-timers Allyson, Annemarie, and Galen for an endless supply of hugs, dark chocolate, and anti-nausea medication; my teachers, Austin Gisriel and Mary Quattlebaum; my big sis, Heidi Potterfield, who is in many ways a superhero, even without the cape and goggles; the Thundering Herd: Sam, Anna, Lily, Nate, Olivia, and Ella; and especially Andy, who patiently put up with my Fiona-size antics and drama over the last two years, cheering me on and faithfully bringing me mugs of hot tea with honey.

Real high cancan leg kicks (with pointed toes) go to my editor, Kate Angelella, who somehow, some way saw something in Fiona even before I knew quite what to do with her, and took a chance on us both.

Read more about Fiona's
not-so-ordinary adventures in

Miss Matched

Fiona Finkelstein had a bad feeling.

It was the kind of feeling she got when she just knew that Mrs. Miltenberger packed a corned beef sandwich in her lunchbox, even though she's told her a gazillion times that she HATES corned beef more than she HATES anything else. Especially after learning that there was actually no corn in it. If there was one thing Fiona flat-out could not stand, it was food that lies.

Fiona didn't know exactly why she was having this feeling today. Maybe because today was the day Mr. Bland, her fourth-grade teacher, was going to draw names for new classroom jobs. For months, Fiona wanted to be picked for electrician. But no matter how tightly she crossed her fingers, Mr. Bland always pulled somebody else's name out of the bucket.

She tapped her green Thinking Pencil on her desk and looked at her best friend, Cleo Button, and Harold Chutney next to her. "I've decided if I don't get to be electrician this time, I'm going to stop taking baths."

"What will that do?" asked Cleo.

"I'll have so much stink on me that Mr. Bland will have to give me the job next time," said Fiona. "I'll tell him that he'll be smelling my stink until he pulls my name out of that bucket."

"Good idea," said Cleo, cracking her knuckles. "I hope I get to be line leader."

Harold pulled his finger out of his nose. "I want to be gardener."

"Gardener?" said Fiona and Cleo at the same time.

"Oh, Boise Idaho. What?" said Harold.

"That's the worst job there is," said Fiona. "There's only one plant that you get to water, and it's a cactus."

Harold shrugged. "What's so great about being electrician?"

Fiona shook her head. "It's only the best job ever. You get to plug in the TV and overhead projector. And work the DVD player."

"And turn off the lights," said Cleo, who was electrician the time before last.

"So?" said Harold, wiping his finger under his desk.

Fiona sighed. Besides being a nose-picker, Harold was the only kid she knew who said things like "Oh, Boise Idaho" and who didn't like cool things like plugs. Sometimes Fiona thought about the possibility that Harold was really an old lady disguised in a boy suit.

The bell rang just then. "Everybody quiet

down," said Mr. Bland. "Before we get started, Principal Sterling is here with an important announcement."

"Good morning, everyone," said Principal Sterling. Her high heels clicked as she walked to the front of the classroom. A boy trailed close behind. He was tall and had spiky hair that made him even taller. "I'd like to introduce a new student who is joining your class." She put her hand on the boy's shoulder. "This is Milo Bridgewater, and he's just moved here to Maryland all the way from Minnesota."

The new boy, Milo, stuffed his hands into his pockets and looked down at his feet. Fiona was trying to remember where Minnesota was because there were lots of M-states and she got them all mixed up. It occurred to her then that Milo also starts with *M* and wasn't that funny. Fiona wondered why there weren't any states that started with *F* and wasn't that unfair. And then she thought of one. "Florida!" she shouted in excitement.

Everyone looked at her. And then they cracked up. Except for Mr. Bland and Principal Sterling. And Minnesota Milo.

Fiona looked around. "Did I say that out loud?"

"Apparently," said Mr. Bland, clearing his throat. "Is there something you wanted to say about Florida?"

"I was just thinking how Florida begins with *F* like Fiona," she explained, "the same way that Minnesota begins with an *M* like, you know, Milo?" Fiona's voice got softer as she got to the end of her explanation and realized how dumb she sounded. Why was it that the thoughts in her head seemed really smart until she said them out loud?

Everybody laughed again. Except for Mr. Bland and Principal Sterling. And Milo. They just stared at her.

Mr. Bland took a deep breath and sighed. Then he shook Milo's hand and said, "Welcome to Ordinary Elementary." He pointed to the empty desk next to Fiona's. "You can take your seat there."

As Milo reached his desk, he looked at Fiona and scowled. Fiona didn't know what she had done to deserve such a look from somebody she hadn't even talked to yet. But since she was not the kind of girl to let a scowl go unanswered, she shot back with an over-the-shoulder Doom Scowl, with medium doom.

"We're finishing up a lesson on measurements, and I'm afraid we won't have your books until later this week," Mr. Bland said to Milo. "But in the meantime, why don't you share with your neighbor?"

Milo looked at Fiona. He shook his head and then turned around to Harold Chutney at the desk behind him.

"Oh, Boise Idaho," said Harold, rubbing his nose, "you want to share with me?"

"I guess," said Milo.

"Cool beans," said Harold. "I like your hairdo. How do you get it to stand up——"

"Milo," said Mr. Bland, "you won't be able to see the chalkboard if you're turned around like that. Share with Fiona."

"Ugh," said Milo.

They grow them rotten in Minnesota, Fiona thought.

Milo moved his chair slowly toward Fiona. She moved her math book exactly one-half inch in Milo's direction. That was as far as she was going to go.

All during math, Milo turned the pages of Fiona's book before she was ready. And each time she turned them back, he mumbled something under his breath. Something that Fiona couldn't quite make out. Which made her grit her teeth.

The second math was over, Fiona pulled her

book away, slammed it shut, and shoved it into her desk. Then she raised her hand. She couldn't wait any longer. "When are you going to draw names for classroom jobs?" she asked when Mr. Bland called on her.

Mr. Bland sighed. "Fiona, whatever would I do without you?" Only he didn't say it in a cursive-letters-on-a-greeting-card kind of way. He said it in a way that made her think Mr. Bland knew exactly what he would do without her.

"And so I don't have to hear you ask a fourth time today," he said, "let's go ahead and draw the names now. But first we need to let Milo put his name in a bucket."

"Oh," said Fiona. She wasn't counting on that.

"Milo," said Mr. Bland, "there are several jobs available in this classroom. Courier, gardener, accountant, and so on. If you see a job you'd like to do, put your name on a piece of paper and drop it into that bucket. Each month we draw a new name."

Milo went over to the Job Center. Fiona chewed on her Thinking Pencil as she watched Milo read the duties listed under each job. He took a gazillion years. Finally, he wrote his name on a slip of paper and dropped it into the bucket marked ELECTRICIAN.

Rotten.

"And now for the big moment," said Mr. Bland, reaching into the first bucket marked COURIER. Fiona was busy crossing each of her fingers while Mr. Bland read off the names in each bucket. Only one bucket mattered to her.

"And lastly, classroom electrician," said Mr. Bland.

"Wait!" Fiona said, as her pinkie slipped off her ring finger. She quickly recrossed them. "Okay, now I'm ready." She watched Mr. Bland pull out a piece of paper and unfold it. As she watched, the corned beef feeling got so strong she could almost smell it.

Mr. Bland held up the paper. "Our new electrician is . . ." Fiona squeezed her crossed fingers tighter and whispered her own name. ". . . Milo Bridgewater."

Enjoy this sweet treat
from Aladdin!

NOW AVAILABLE

FROM ALADDIN
PUBLISHED BY SIMON & SCHUSTER

Nancy Drew and the Clue Crew

Test your detective skills with more Clue Crew cases!

FROM ALADDIN • PUBLISHED BY SIMON & SCHUSTER

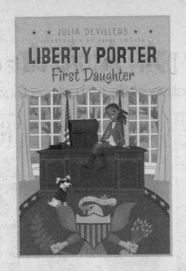

Life in the White House
will never be the same!